He took both her hands in his large ones and dragged her to him....

She felt herself melt into his arms, his mouth warm, his lips strong and sure. It swept her up like an adventure where anything was possible.

Jud pulled her closer, melding their bodies together as he explored her mouth, his hands tangled in her hair, his body hard and possessive.

When he finally let her come up for air, she was breathing hard, heart racing, traitorous body crying out for more. The pickup's windows were steamed over even though the pickup was still running, the heater working hard as it could to clear the glass.

The outside world appeared to be lost, which was just fine with her. She never wanted to leave this pickup cab or this man's arms....

B.J. DANIELS

HUNTING DOWN *the* HORSEMAN

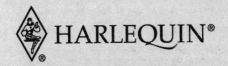

HARLEQUIN®

TORONTO • NEW YORK • LONDON
AMSTERDAM • PARIS • SYDNEY • HAMBURG
STOCKHOLM • ATHENS • TOKYO • MILAN • MADRID
PRAGUE • WARSAW • BUDAPEST • AUCKLAND

I always wanted a sister, but my mother didn't cooperate. So I'm not sure how it was that I came to write a book about sisters. But I did. Fortunately, I have two women in my life who have been like sisters—sister-in-laws who also became good friends. That's why this book is dedicated to Frances Demarais and Annie Rissman for being the sisters I never had.

ISBN-13: 978-0-373-69398-6
ISBN-10:   0-373-69398-2

HUNTING DOWN THE HORSEMAN

Recycling programs
for this product may
not exist in your area.

www.eHarlequin.com

Printed in U.S.A.

ABOUT THE AUTHOR

B.J. Daniels wrote her first book after a career as an award-winning newspaper journalist and author of 37 published short stories. That first book, *Odd Man Out*, received a 4½ star review from *Romantic Times BOOKreviews* magazine and went on to be nominated for Best Intrigue for that year. Since then she has won numerous awards including a career achievement award for romantic suspense and numerous nominations and awards for best book.

Daniels lives in Montana with her husband, Parker, and two springer spaniels, Spot and Jem. When she isn't writing, she snowboards, camps, boats and plays tennis. Daniels is a member of Mystery Writers of America, Sisters in Crime, Thriller Writers, Kiss of Death and Romance Writers of America.

To contact her, write B.J. Daniels, P.O. Box 1173, Malta, MT 59538, or e-mail her at bjdaniels@mtintouch.net. Check out her Web site, www.bjdaniels.com.

Books by B.J. Daniels

HARLEQUIN INTRIGUE

803—COWBOY ACCOMPLICE*
845—AMBUSHED!*
851—HIGH-CALIBER COWBOY*
857—SHOTGUN SURRENDER*
876—WHEN TWILIGHT COMES
897—CRIME SCENE AT
    CARDWELL RANCH**
915—SECRET WEAPON SPOUSE
936—UNDENIABLE PROOF
953—KEEPING CHRISTMAS**
969—BIG SKY STANDOFF**
996—SECRET OF
    DEADMAN'S COULEE†
1002—THE NEW DEPUTY
    IN TOWN†
1024—THE MYSTERY MAN
    OF WHITEHORSE†

1030—CLASSIFIED
    CHRISTMAS†
1053—MATCHMAKING WITH
    A MISSION†
1059—SECOND CHANCE
    COWBOY†
1083—MONTANA ROYALTY†
1125—SHOTGUN BRIDE††
1131—HUNTING DOWN THE
    HORSEMAN††

*McCalls' Montana
**Montana Mystique
†Whitehorse, Montana
††Whitehorse, Montana:
  The Corbetts

CAST OF CHARACTERS

Jud Corbett—The stuntman had his life planned, until he saw the Montana cowgirl ride.

Faith Bailey—The cowgirl would take on any challenge, whether it was a handsome stuntman who knew her desires, or a killer.

Erik Zander—The director had too many skeletons in his closet. One was bound to get out with deadly consequences.

Chantal Lee—The leading lady always got what she wanted. But what was she after this time?

Brooke Keith—The stuntwoman never got her man. This time she was hoping the film would have a different ending.

Nancy Davis—Could the mousy assistant director be hiding more than her figure behind her dowdy clothing and bad haircut?

Keyes Hasting—He knew what money and power could buy and planned to use both to get what he wanted.

Nevada Wells—The leading man resented Jud Corbett getting the spotlight.

Eve Bailey Jackson—She thought she'd never know the truth about her birth until a stranger came to town with a tragic story of love and loss.

Sheriff Carter Jackson—He had every reason to be concerned about the trouble the Bailey girls were getting into now.

Chapter One

According to the legend, the town of Lost Creek is cursed. Only a few buildings remain along the shore of the Missouri River in an isolated part of Montana.

The story told over the years is that a band of outlaws rode into the fledgling town and killed a mother and child, while the rest of the residents watched from a safe distance.

When the husband returned, he found his wife lying dead in the dirt street, his child and her doll lying next to her, and the townspeople still hiding from the outlaws.

He picked up his daughter's doll from the dirt and swore revenge on the townspeople.

One by one, residents began to find a small cloth doll on their doorsteps—and then they'd die. According to one story, the rest of the townspeople fled for their lives.

But another story tells of a pile of bones found at the bottom of a cave years later. Men, women and children's bones—the residents of Lost Creek and evidence of a story of true retribution.

THE SUN SINKING into the Little Rockies, Jud Corbett spurred his horse as he raced through the narrow canyon. Behind him he could hear the thunder of horses growing louder. The marshal star he wore on his leather vest caught the light as the canyon heat rose in waves, making the towering rock walls shimmer. Sweat trickled down his back. His mouth went dry.

Just a little farther.

His horse stumbled as he rounded the last bend and almost went down. He'd lost precious seconds. The riders were close behind him. If his horse had fallen…

His gray Stetson pulled down low over his dark hair, he burst from the canyon. On the horizon, the ghost town of Lost Creek wavered like a mirage under the cloudless blue of Montana's big sky.

Jud felt his heart leap as he spurred his horse to even more speed, adrenaline coursing through his veins.

Almost there.

The loud report of a rifle shot punctuated the air. Jud grabbed his side, doubling over and grimacing with pain. The second shot caught him in the back.

Tumbling headlong from his horse, he hit the ground in a cloud of dust.

"Cut! That's a wrap."

FROM THE SIDELINES, assistant director Nancy Davis watched Jud Corbett get up grinning to retrieve his Stetson from the dirt.

"He's such a showoff," stuntwoman Brooke Keith said beside her, her tone a mixture of envy and awe.

"The man just loves his work," Nancy said, cutting her gaze to the stuntwoman and body double.

That got a chuckle from Brooke. "Kind of like the way the leading lady just likes to be *friendly.*"

Nancy watched as Chantal Lee sauntered over to Jud and, standing on tiptoes, whispered something in his ear.

Jud let loose that famous grin of his as Chantal brushed her lips against the stuntman's suntanned cheek before she sauntered away, her hips swaying provocatively.

"Easy," Nancy warned.

"Easy is exactly what she is," Brooke said with obvious disgust as she walked off toward Jud.

Jud Corbett was shaking his head in obvious amusement at Chantal. Whatever she'd offered him, he wasn't taking the bait.

As Brooke joined Jud, Nancy couldn't help the sliver of worry that wedged itself just under her skin. All she needed was Chantal and Brooke at each other's throats. There was enough animosity between them as it was. She'd have to talk to Chantal and tell her to tone it down.

As for Brooke... Nancy watched the stuntwoman sidle up to Jud and knew the signs only too well. A catfight was brewing, and Jud was about to be caught right in the middle. Nancy wondered if he realized yet what a dangerous position he was in.

"NICE STUNT," Brooke said with an edge to her voice as she handed Jud a bottle of water.

"Thanks," he said and took a long drink. "But you could have done that stunt blindfolded."

She smiled at that, but the smile never reached her eyes. "I was referring to Chantal's stunt."

"I hadn't noticed." He'd noticed, though he certainly hadn't taken it seriously. Chantal liked to stir things up.

Brooke chuckled. "You noticed."

"Good thing I never date women I work with while on a film."

Brooke eyed him. "That's your rule?"

"The Corbett Code," Jud said, lifting his right hand as if swearing in.

She laughed. He liked Brooke. He'd worked on a couple of films with her. She was a grown-up tomboy.

Chantal Lee, on the other hand, was a blue-eyed blond beauty, all legs, bulging bosom and flowing golden hair. While Brooke was the perfect stunt double for the star, she dressed in a way that played down her curves. The two could have passed for sisters, but they were as different as sugar and salt.

Brooke was scowling in the direction of Chantal's trailer. "Did you know Chantal demanded another stunt-woman and body double? Zander refused, even though Chantal threatened to break her contract."

That surprised Jud. Not about Chantal, but about director Erik Zander, who had never seemed like a man with much backbone. But if the rumors were true, Zander was betting everything on this film, a Western thriller. Apparently, it was do or die at this point in his career.

According to the rumor mill, the director was in debt up to his eyeballs from legal fees after a young starlet had drowned in his pool and the autopsy showed that the woman was chockfull of drugs—and pregnant with Zander's baby.

He'd managed to keep from getting arrested, but it had cost him not just his small fortune but his fiancée, the daughter of a wealthy film producer. She broke their engagement, and that was the end of her wealthy father backing Zander's films.

Jud paid little attention to rumors but he did have to wonder why Erik Zander had decided to produce and direct *Death at Lost Creek,* given the publicity after the death at his beach house. On top of that, Zander had cast Chantal

Lee and Nevada Wells, former lovers who'd just gone through a very nasty public breakup. Jud feared that would be the kiss of the death for this film.

Jud had gotten roped into the job because Zander had made him an offer he couldn't refuse—complete control over all the stunts in the movie as stunt coordinator.

Suddenly Chantal's trailer door slammed open. The star burst from it, clutching something in her hand as she made a beeline for them.

As she drew closer, Jud saw that the star had one of the small rag dolls from the film gripped in her fist. She stalked up to the two of them and thrust the doll into Brooke's face.

"I know you left this on my bed, you bitch!" Chantal screamed. "If I catch you in my trailer again…" She threw the doll at Brooke.

Jud watched Chantal storm away. Everyone in the common area had witnessed the scene but now pretended to go back to what they were doing.

Beside him, Brooke stooped to pick up the doll that had landed at her feet.

Jud saw at once that the doll wasn't one from the prop department. He took the tiny rag doll from her. It was so crudely made that there was something obscene about it.

Brooke wiped her hands down the sides of her jeans as if regretting touching the ugly thing. "I didn't put that on her bed." She sounded confused and maybe a little scared.

"You're not buying into that local legend," he said with a chuckle. "Not you."

She smiled at that but still appeared upset. According to the script for *Death at Lost Creek* and local legend, the recipient of one of these dolls was either about to have some really bad luck, or die.

"I'll take that," Nancy snapped as she came up to them and held out her hand.

Jud dropped the tiny rag doll into it. From the look on the assistant director's face she was not amused. But then Jud didn't think he'd seen her smile since he'd gotten to the set.

"I can't wait until this is over," Brooke said, her voice breaking after Nancy walked away. "I hate this place."

He'd heard the crew complaining about the isolation since the closest town was Whitehorse, Montana, which rolled up its sidewalks by eight o'clock every night.

But Jud suspected it was the script—not the location— that was really getting to them. Their trailers were circled like wagon trains, one circle for the crew, another for the upper echelon in what was called the base camp.

Not far from the circled RVs was the catering tent and beyond it was the false fronts and main street depicting the infamous town of Lost Creek.

But it was the real town of Lost Creek farther down the canyon that had everyone spooked. Now a ghost town deep in the badlands of the Missouri Breaks, with its history it was a real-life horror story.

All that was left of the town were a few rotting wooden buildings along the creek and the Missouri River. The town, like so many others, had been started by settlers coming by riverboats up the wide Missouri to settle Montana.

The wild, isolated country itself was difficult enough for the settlers. The river had cut thousands of deep ravines into the expanse, leaving behind outcroppings of rocks and scrub pine and hidden canyons where a person could get lost forever. Some had.

But even more dangerous were the outlaws who hid in the badlands of the Breaks and attacked the riverboats— and the towns. Lost Creek had been one of those towns.

"I have to get away from here for a while," Brooke said suddenly. "Are you going into town tonight?"

"Sorry, I've been summoned to a family dinner at the ranch. Which means something is up, or I'd ask you to come along."

"That's right, your family lives near here now. Trails West Ranch, right?"

He nodded, wondering how she knew that. But it wasn't exactly a secret given who his father was. Grayson Corbett had graced the cover of several national magazines for his work with conservation easements both in Texas and Montana.

"I'm dreading dinner tonight," Jud admitted. He had been ever since he'd gotten the call from his father's new wife, Kate. That in itself didn't bode well. Normally Grayson would have called his son himself. Clearly Kate had extended the invitation to make it harder for Jud to decline.

"Family," Brooke said. "That's all there is, huh."

"Are you sure you're all right?"

She smiled. "I'm fine. You're a nice man, Jud Corbett, but don't worry, I won't let it get around."

He watched her walk away, strangely uneasy. He'd worked with Brooke before. She was a beautiful, talented woman with a core of steel—much like Chantal. She didn't scare easily. He suspected whatever was bothering her had nothing to do with a silly rag doll or the horror stories that went with it.

BABY SHOWERS were enough to make any twentysomething female nervous. For Faith Bailey it was pure torture. But she had no choice.

This was a joint shower for the very pregnant Cavanaugh sisters, who Faith had grown up with.

Laci Cavanaugh had married Bridger Duvall, and the two owned the Northern Lights Restaurant in downtown Whitehorse. Laney Cavanaugh had married Deputy Sheriff Nick Giovanni, and they had built a home near Old Town Whitehorse, where the girls' grandparents lived. Both sisters were due any day now—and looked it.

The shower was being held at the Bailey Ranch in Old Town Whitehorse, the only place Faith had ever considered home in her twenty-six years. Another reason Faith had to be here.

But as she sat in her own ranch house living room, she couldn't help feeling out of place. Almost all of her close friends were married now, except for Georgia Michaels, who owned the knitting shop in town, In Stitches. And everyone knew what followed marriage: a baby carriage.

"Can you believe this population explosion?" her friend Georgia whispered. On the other side of Georgia, their good friend Rory Buchanan Barrow was fighting morning sickness even though it was afternoon.

When they were all kids, growing up in this isolated part of Montana, they'd all vowed not to get married until they were at least thirty-five, and none of them was going to stick around Whitehorse. Instead, they'd sworn they would see the world, have exciting adventures and date men they hadn't grown up with all their lives and dated since junior high.

While some hadn't married the boy next door, they'd all fallen hard for their men and totally changed their big plans for the future.

Faith couldn't help but feel annoyed with them as she looked around the crowded living room and saw so many protruding bellies and wedding bands. To make matters worse, they all looked ecstatically happy.

A man and marriage just wasn't Faith Bailey's secret

desire, she thought as she looked wistfully out the window at the rolling grassland and the rugged edge of the Missouri Breaks in the distance.

"I had to add a baby bootie knitting class at the shop," Georgia whispered to her. "Something about getting pregnant makes a woman want to knit. It's *really* spooky."

Faith laughed, imagining her sister McKenna knitting booties in the near future. McKenna had started her Paint horse farm, and her husband, Nate, was busy building them a home on a hill overlooking the place, but neither had made a secret of their plans to start a family right away.

It was her older sister, Eve, who Faith thought would be hesitant. While all three Bailey sisters were adopted and not related by blood, Eve was the one who was driven to find her birth mother. Before bringing a child into the world, Eve would be more determined than ever to know about her genes and the blood that ran through her veins.

Faith watched Laci and Laney open one beautifully wrapped box after another of darling baby clothing and the latest in high-tech baby supplies, all the time wishing she was out riding her horse. After all, she was only home for the summer, and she'd promised herself she was going to spend every waking moment in the saddle.

"If I see one more breast pump, I'm going to be sick," she whispered to Georgia who laughed and whispered back, "Do you have any idea what some of that stuff is for?"

Before Faith could tell her she didn't have a clue, Laci's water broke, and not two seconds later, so did Laney's.

Faith smiled to herself. She was going to get in that ride today after all.

SHOWERED AND CHANGED, Jud came out of his trailer to find Chantal Lee waiting for him beside his pickup. He groaned under his breath as he noticed Nevada Wells sitting in the shade of his trailer with a half-empty bottle of bourbon on the table next to him. Nevada was watching Chantal with a look of unadulterated hatred on his face.

The two stars had made front-page tabloid news for months beginning with their scorching affair, their torrid public shows of affection and their scandalous breakup—all in public.

Jud wondered what director Erik Zander had been thinking, throwing the two together in this Western thriller, given their recent past. How were they going to get an audience to believe they were crazy about each other in this film and not just plain crazy?

As Jud neared his pickup, Chantal sidled up to him in a cloud of expensive perfume and a revealing dress that accented her every asset. She looped her arms around his neck and smiled up at him.

Across the compound, Nevada grabbed up his bourbon bottle and stormed into his trailer.

"If you're trying to make Nevada jealous," Jud said to Chantal, "you can stop now. He's gone back into his trailer."

"Don't you read the tabloids?" she asked as he disengaged her from around his neck. "I've moved on. So," she said, "how about showing me the town tonight?"

"Whitehorse? As flattering as the offer is, I'm afraid I have other plans."

"Brooke." Chantal made a face as she said the stunt-woman's name.

He shook his head, knowing whatever fueled this battle between the two women had started long before now. "I don't date anyone I work with during filming. I'm having dinner with my family."

Chantal brightened. "Take *me*," she pleaded. "I am

bored beyond belief out here in the middle of nowhere. You'll be saving my life."

"Sorry," he said, thinking about what would happen if he took her home with him. He'd dodged a bullet by sacrificing his brother Shane to the marriage pact he and his four brothers had made. But he was still in the line of fire.

It would be fun, though, to see his family's expressions if he pretended interest in Chantal for a wife. But even he couldn't do that to them.

No, the last thing he wanted was to call attention to himself right now. He'd hoped that karma would be on his side when he and his brothers had drawn straws to see who would have to find a wife first. Then he'd drawn the shortest straw and known he had to do something fast, so he had. He'd found the perfect woman—for his brother Shane.

That little maneuver had really only delayed the problem, though. Jud knew in his heart that what his father wanted wasn't so much for each of his sons to marry but for them to settle in Montana closer to Trails West Ranch, the ranch Grayson Corbett had bought for his new bride, Kate.

Grayson was no fool. He had to know that getting all his sons to settle down in Montana probably wasn't going to happen, no matter what kind of carrot he dangled in front of them. But it *was* some carrot.

Grayson's first wife, the boys' mother, had written five letters, one to each son, before she died. The letters, only recently found, were to be read on each son's wedding day. Her dying wish in a letter to Grayson was that the boys would marry by the age of thirty-five—and all marry a Montana cowgirl.

It was hard to go against the dying wishes of his mother, even a mother Jud, the youngest, couldn't remember, since she'd died not long after he and his twin brother, Dalton, were born. Being a Corbett demanded that he go along with the marriage pact the five brothers had made—and eventually live up to the deal.

The problem was that he'd never met anyone he wanted to date more than a few times, let alone marry.

But then most of the women he knew were like Chantal, he thought, as beside him she pretended to pout.

"You're going to hate yourself in the morning for leaving me behind," she cooed.

Jud nodded ruefully. "Ain't that the truth."

"Your loss," she said, and turned in a huff to storm off, again putting a whole lot of movement into those hips of hers.

Jud smiled as he headed for his pickup. He had a weakness for beautiful women and a whole lot of oats left to sow, but his real-life exploits could never live up to those that showed up in the movie magazines about him.

When he thought about it, what woman in her right mind would want to marry a man who did dangerous stunts for living? And he had no intention of quitting until he was too old to climb into the saddle, he thought, as he headed for the ranch.

FAITH BAILEY RODE her horse to the spot where she always went when she wanted to make sure no one saw what she was up to. She'd been coming here since she was a girl. It was far enough from the ranch house and yet not too far away should she need help.

As she got ready, she recalled too vividly the time she'd taken a tumble and broken her arm.

"Were you thrown from your horse?" her mother had demanded when she returned to the house holding her arm after one of her "rides."

Not exactly. "All of a sudden I was on the ground,"

Faith had said, determined not to lie—but at the same time, not about to tell the whole truth, which she'd feared would get her banned from horseback riding altogether.

She'd kept the truth from even her two older sisters, Eve and McKenna. They couldn't have kept her secret, afraid she'd break her fool neck and they'd get blamed for it.

Now with her mother remarried and living in Florida, Faith still didn't like to upset her family. They'd all been through enough without that. So she kept her trick riding to herself. It was her little secret—just like her heart's desire.

Faith had taken more precautions after the broken arm incident, and while she'd gotten hurt occasionally as she'd grown older, she'd also kept that to herself.

She made a few runs along a flat spot at the far end of a pasture before she got her horse up to a gallop and slipped her boots from the stirrups to climb up onto the back of the horse behind the saddle.

It was a balancing act. Standing, she galloped across the flat area of pasture, feeling the wind in her face and the exhilaration. She always started with this trick, then moved on to the harder ones.

Her mind was on the task at hand. Over the galloping of her horse, the pounding of her heart and the rush of adrenaline racing through her veins, Faith didn't hear the sound of the vehicle come up the dirt road and stop.

JUD CORBETT BLINKED, telling himself he wasn't seeing a woman standing on the back of a horse galloping across the landscape.

He'd stopped his pickup and now watched with growing fascination. The young woman seemed oblivious to everything but the stunt, her head high, long blond hair blowing back, the sun firing it to spun gold.

She still hadn't seen him and didn't seem to notice as he climbed out of his truck and walked over to lean against the jackleg fence to watch her go from one trick to another with both proficiency and confidence.

He'd seen his share of stuntmen and women do the same tricks. But this young woman had a style and grace and determination that mesmerized him.

She reminded him of himself. He'd started on the road to his career as a kid doing every horseback trick he could think of on his family's ranch in Texas. He'd hit the dirt more times than he wanted to remember and had the healed broken bones to prove it.

The young woman pulled off a difficult trick with effortless efficiency, but as she slowed her horse, he could see that she still wasn't quite happy with it and intended to try the stunt again.

"Hey," he called to her as he leaned on the fence.

Her head came up, and, although he couldn't see her face in the shadow of her Western hat brim, he saw that he'd startled her. She'd thought she was all alone.

"Didn't mean to scare you," he said, shoving back his hat and smiling over at her. "On that last trick, try staying a little farther forward next time. It will help with your balance. I'm Jud Corbett, by the way." No reaction. "The stuntman?"

She cocked her head at him and he thought as she spurred her horse that she intended to ride over to the fence to talk to him.

Instead, she turned her horse and took off at a gallop down the fence line. He knew what she planned to do the moment she reined in. She shoved down her Western straw hat and came racing back toward him.

This time the trick was flawless—right up until the end.

He saw her shoot him a satisfied look an instant before she lost her balance. She tumbled from the horse, hitting the dirt in a cloud of dust.

Chapter Two

Jud scrambled over the fence and ran to the young woman lying on the ground, wishing he'd just kept his big mouth shut and left her alone.

She lay flat on her back in the dirt, her long, blond hair over her face.

"Are you all right?" he cried as he dropped to his knees next to her. She didn't answer, but he could see the rise and fall of her chest and knew she was still breathing.

Quickly, he brushed her hair back from her face to reveal a pair of beautiful blue eyes—and drew back in surprise as one of those eyes winked at him and a smile curled the bow-shaped lips.

From a distance, he'd taken her for a teenager. Even up close she had that look: blond, blue-eyed, freckled. Now, though, he saw that she was closer to his own age.

His heart kicked up a beat, but no longer from fear for her safety. "You did that on purpose!"

She chuckled and shoved herself up on her elbows to grin at him. "You think?"

He wanted to throttle her, but her grin was contagious. "Okay, maybe I deserved it."

"You did," she said without hesitation.

"I was just trying to help." He'd seen so much potential in her and had wanted to— What had he wanted to do? Take her under his wing?

That was when he thought she was a teenager. Now he would have preferred taking her in his arms.

Rising, he offered her a hand up from the ground. She stared at his open palm for a moment, then reached up to clasp his hand. Hers was small, lightly callused and warm. He drew her up, feeling strangely awkward around her. The woman was a spitfire.

She drew her hand back from his, scooped up her Western hat from the dirt and began to slap it against her jean-clad long legs, dust rising as she studied him as if she didn't quite trust him. She didn't trust *him?*

"Look, I feel like we got off on the wrong foot," Jud said as she shoved the cowboy hat down on her blond head again. "How can I make it up to you?"

She grinned. "Oh, you've more than made it up to me, Mr. Corbett." She whistled for her horse and the mare came trotting over. As she swung up into the saddle, she said, "Thanks for the *tip.*"

He couldn't help smiling at the sarcasm lacing her tone and wished he wasn't so damned intrigued by her. She was cocky and self-assured and wasn't in the least impressed with him. It left him feeling a little off balance since he'd always thought he had a way with women.

She reined her horse around to leave.

"Wait. Would you like to have breakfast?"

She drew her horse up and glanced back at him. *"Breakfast?"*

He realized belatedly how she'd taken the invitation. Since he was tied up for dinner tonight, his first thought had been breakfast.

"I already have plans for dinner tonight, but I was thinking—"

"I can well imagine what you were thinking." She spurred her horse and left him standing in the dust.

He watched her ride away, trying to remember the last time he'd been turned down so completely. It wasn't until she'd dropped over the horizon that he realized he didn't even know her name.

FAITH FELT LIGHT-HEADED. She couldn't wipe the grin off her face or banish the excitement that rippled through her as she rode her horse back to her family ranch house.

Jud Corbett. The most notorious stuntman in Hollywood. There wasn't a stunt he couldn't do on a horse. And he had seen her ride!

She chuckled to herself at the memory of his expression when she'd winked at him. She hadn't been able to help herself. She'd wanted to show off. She was lucky she hadn't broken her fool neck doing it, though.

Her heart had been pounding in her chest when she opened her eyes fully and had seen him in the flesh. The Hollywood movie and stuntman magazines hadn't done Jud Corbett justice. The man, who'd made a name for himself not only for his stunts, but also as a ladies' man, was *gorgeous*.

He'd taken her breath away more than her pratfall. She knew about the film being shot down in the Breaks since her sister McKenna was providing some of the horses.

But Faith had never dreamt she'd get the chance to meet Jud Corbett—let alone be asked to breakfast, even though she knew what *that* meant, given his reputation.

What had he been doing on that old road, anyway? No one used it. Or at least she'd thought that was true. Wait a minute. That road led to the Trails West Ranch property, and hadn't she heard that someone named Grayson Corbett had bought it?

Corbett. Of course. She'd just never put two and two together. Jud must be one of Grayson Corbett's five sons she'd been hearing about. Which meant Jud was on his way to the ranch when he'd seen her.

Her grin spread wider. She still couldn't believe it. She'd fooled the legendary Jud Corbett with one of her tricks.

As she neared the house, she tried to compose herself. Her older sister Eve's pickup was parked out front. Faith would have loved to burst into the house and tell Eve all about her afternoon. But this didn't seem the time to reveal her trick-riding secret. Eve worried about her enough as it was, and Eve had her own concerns right now.

Faith knew not wanting to worry her family wasn't the only reason she'd kept her secret. It was *hers,* all hers. Growing up, she was always lumped with her sisters as one of the wild Bailey girls. Eve and McKenna had been stubborn, independent and outspoken.

Faith herself had been all of those and then some, but she'd thought her trick riding as a girl had made her the true daring one.

And now Jud Corbett, of all people, knew.

She tried to assure herself that he wouldn't tell anyone. Who *could* he tell? He probably didn't even know who she was—or care. Faith tried to relax as she took care of her horse, then walked up to the house, only a little sore from her stunts.

"Everything all right?" Eve asked from the front porch.

Faith hadn't seen her sister sitting on the swing in the shade. Eve lived with her husband, Sheriff Carter Jackson, down the road, but she spent a lot of time in the family ranch house when Faith was home, acting as surrogate mother since their mother had remarried and moved to Florida.

"I didn't see you there," Faith said as she mounted the steps.

Eve was studying her. "You look flushed. Are you feeling all right?"

"Great." It was true. "I wish you wouldn't worry about me, though." Also true, but she hadn't meant the words to come out so sharply. At twenty-six, she was too old to be mothered by her thirty-three-year-old big sister. But mostly, she didn't like worrying Eve.

Eve's silence surprised her—as well as what she saw her sister holding on her lap.

"Is that your baby quilt?" Faith asked, frowning. "Does this mean…?"

Eve shook her head. "I'm not ready to have a baby yet."

"Well, you're the only one in the county," Faith said, dropping onto the swing beside her. "Have you heard if Laci and Laney had their babies yet?"

Eve shook her head, fingering the quilt on her lap. "I was just thinking about *my* biological mother and the night she gave birth to me and Bridger."

Faith had hoped that once Eve was married to the only man she'd ever loved, she might not need to keep up her search. Eve and her twin brother, Bridger, had only been reunited a year ago, brought together by the mutual need to find the woman who'd given them up.

"We know her name," Eve said, surprising Faith. "It's Constance Small."

"You found her?" Faith asked, shocked.

"Not yet. All we have so far is a name and a little information. She was seventeen, possibly a runaway. She disappeared right after she gave birth to us."

"I'm sorry." Faith, like her sisters, was also adopted, but she had no desire to know her birth mother or the circumstances. She couldn't understand Eve's need. Clearly, it could lead to disappointment—if not worse.

Eve put the quilt aside. "Are you sure you're all right? Stay here in the shade. I'll get you some lemonade."

Faith laughed, glad that her sister had something to keep her mind off finding Constance Small. "Thanks, but I just need a shower."

"You haven't forgotten the fund-raiser tonight at the community center, have you?"

Faith had. She frantically searched around for a way to get out of it.

"Don't even think about backing out," Eve said. "McKenna called a little while ago to make sure we were both going."

Faith groaned at the thought of going to the dance.

"Faith?" her sister said in a voice that reminded Faith of her mother's.

"Of course I'm going." She couldn't let her sisters down. Even though they weren't blood related, there was a bond between them that nothing could break.

"Wear your red dress."

Not even the thought of a county dance could dampen Faith's mood for long. As she went into the house she hugged her latest secret to her, treasuring what had happened this afternoon.

But minutes later as she stepped into the shower, Faith realized that Jud Corbett had awakened something inside her. A secret impossible desire that she'd put away the same way she'd put away her dolls and her childhood daydreams.

Like a genie freed from its bottle, her secret yearning

had emerged now and, even if Faith had wanted to, she knew no matter how dangerous, it wasn't going back into that bottle.

JUD OPENED the front door of the Trails West Ranch house and breathed in the mouthwatering scents of chile rellenos, homemade refried beans and freshly fried corn tortillas with Juanita's special spices. He'd bet she'd made flan for dessert.

His favorite meal. He closed his eyes, pausing to hang up his jacket and brace himself for whatever was awaiting him. The only good news about his father's move to Montana was that he'd somehow talked Juanita into making the move with him and Kate.

The menu alone was a tip-off, even if Jud hadn't seen his brothers' vehicles parked out front. It was just as he'd suspected: a family meeting.

Hearing the tinkle of ice in crystal glasses and the hum of voices in the bar area, Jud headed toward it, pocketing the pleasurable thoughts of the young woman horseback rider he'd seen.

"Jud," his father said as he spotted him. Grayson looked at his watch and frowned. He was a big, handsome, congenial man, as open as the land he lived on.

"Sorry I'm late." Jud thought about mentioning the woman he'd seen but changed his mind. He got razzed enough about women, his own undoing since he'd made the mistake of sharing some of his exploits, embellishing, of course, to make the stories better—just as the movie magazines did.

"Dinner smells amazing," he said, hoping to cut short whatever this summit meeting might be about.

Everyone was gathered in the large family room, a bad sign. His oldest brother Russell stood behind the bar nursing a beer; Lantry was propped on a stool talking to their father's wife, Kate; Shane was sprawled in a chair by the window—no sign of Maddie, his fiancée, another bad sign; and fraternal twin Dalton was whispering with Juanita and stealing tortilla chips from the large bowl in her hands.

"So what's up?" Jud asked as he helped himself to a beer from the bar fridge, just wanting to get this over with.

He saw a look pass between his father and Kate. Uh-oh. He felt his heart dip. For years after their mother, Rebecca, had died, Grayson had been alone. They'd thought he would never remarry.

Then along came Kate. Kate had shown up at their Texas ranch with a box of photographs of their mother. Rebecca had been the ranch manager's daughter. Kate the daughter of the ranch owner. The two had grown up together on Trails West Ranch outside of Whitehorse, Montana.

Kate had lost touch with Rebecca over the years. When she'd found the photographs, she'd said she'd thought enough time had passed since Rebecca's death that Grayson might want them.

He had. And it wasn't long before he'd wanted Kate, as well. All these years Grayson hadn't been able to go through his deceased wife's belongings. With Kate's love and support, he finally had—and found the letters from their mother, triggering this marriage pact among the sons.

Grayson had fallen hard for Kate. So hard that he'd sold his holdings in Texas and bought Kate's long-lost family ranch in Montana as a present for her, then moved them to Montana.

His father had been so happy with Kate. Jud couldn't bear it if that was no longer the case.

"Kate and I have something to tell you," Grayson said now, his expression way too serious for Jud's tastes.

Jud took a swig of his beer and braced himself for the worst. All five brothers had thought their father's marriage and the move to Montana was impulsive and worried, since even Jud had noticed that Kate had seemed different here at the ranch.

She should have been happy to have her family ranch back after it had been lost when her father died. But she hadn't been.

"Kate?" Grayson said, giving his wife's shoulder a squeeze.

She raised her head, glancing around as if looking for someone. Her gaze settled on Shane sitting by the window, his back to them.

What the hell, Jud thought, feeling the tension in the room crank up several notches.

"I have a daughter."

They all stared at Kate, knowing she'd never been married and as far as they'd known had never had a child.

"I gave birth to her when I was in my early twenties, right after my father died, right before I left Montana," Kate said, her voice strong. "I gave her up for adoption when she was only hours old." She swallowed. "I've regretted it ever since."

What was this? True confessions?

"You weren't in any shape to raise a child alone," Grayson said. "You had little choice given your situation."

She cut her eyes to him and he fell silent again. "The father of my child was married." Her back stiffened visibly. "He wasn't going to leave his wife. I was hurt. I told him the baby had died. It wasn't until recently that I told him the truth."

You could have heard a pin drop in the room. Everyone was staring at Kate. Except Shane. His back still to them, he appeared to be gazing out the front window as if uninterested. Or had he already heard this?

Jud felt his chest tighten. "What happened to your baby?"

Kate turned toward him. "Adopted by a local family, she grew up in Old Town Whitehorse."

Jud did the math. "So she would be in her mid-twenties."

"Twenty-six," Kate said.

He could see what was coming. "Does she know who you are?"

Kate nodded.

"Of course, she was surprised," Grayson said. "So it is going to take some time to get to know her and her to know us."

"So when do we get to meet her?" Dalton asked.

The silence said it all.

"You've already met her," Kate said. "Her name is Maddie Cavanaugh."

Jud shot a look at Shane.

"Shane's fiancée?" Lantry demanded, glancing at his older brother, as well. Shane still didn't say anything or look in their direction.

"I take it Maddie is upset," Jud said, stating what he knew was the obvious.

"She'll come around," Grayson said, always the optimist.

"I wanted you all to know so you understood that it might be tense when Maddie is around. She's having trouble forgiving me. I'm having trouble forgiving myself."

For the first time, tears shone in her eyes, but she seemed to hold them back with sheer determination.

"Are you worried about the legal ramifications, Kate?" Lantry asked, always the lawyer.

"No," Grayson said. "She is Kate's daughter and will be treated like any other member of this family."

"But the wedding is still on, right?" Jud asked.

Russell shot him a warning look.

Juanita announced dinner was ready as if on cue, but no one moved.

"This calls for margaritas," Grayson announced.

Kate touched his arm. "Maybe after dinner," she suggested.

Everyone except Shane headed in for dinner. Jud hung back. "I wasn't only thinking of myself just now," he said to Shane.

"I know." Shane got to his feet. "We should join the rest of the family." He looked like hell. Clearly this was taking a toll on him.

"Maddie will come around. You know she will," Jud said. "She loves you. It would be a damned shame if you let this come between you. You're made for each other."

Shane smiled. "Not to mention the pressure it would put on you to tie the knot."

"Yeah," Jud said smiling ruefully. "Not to mention that."

EVE WISHED she didn't know her two younger sisters so well. The moment she'd seen Faith's face on her return from her ride, she'd known something had happened.

Whatever it had been, Faith was keeping it to herself. Eve had noticed right away that Faith had been thrown from her horse. There was dirt ground into the seat of her jeans and into the elbows of her Western shirt.

This wasn't anything new. Over the years Faith had returned many times from rides fighting to hide the fact that she'd been thrown. Often also trying to hide her hurt pride.

This time, however, Faith seemed jubilant, and that had Eve as perplexed as anything. She would have thought a man was involved, but at this point in Faith's life, she seemed to prefer the company of her horse.

Eve looked up at the knock at her screen door to find her twin brother, Bridger, standing just outside. She couldn't help thinking about the first time she'd seen him.

Unlike her, he'd known he was adopted. He'd even known he'd had a twin sister. Their shared blood had thrown them together as they'd tried to find out the truth about their illegal adoptions.

"Hey," he said as he met her gaze through the screen. He was dark haired like her. Eve had always known she was different from her mother, father and two sisters, who all had blond hair and blue eyes. Now she knew why.

"Just the person I wanted to see," she said as he came into the house, and she gave him a hug.

"Faith must be home," he said, glancing at the supper she had started. Eve had remodeled her grandma Nina Mae's home down the road when Nina Mae had to go into the rest home with Alzheimer's.

The Bailey ranch house sat empty except when Faith was home. Eve didn't want her sister, who insisted on staying at the ranch house, to come home to an empty house, so she spent time here trying to make it a home for Faith.

Faith had taken their parents divorce the hardest. Now their father lived in town with his girlfriend and their mother in Florida.

"You're an awfully nice sister," Bridger said as he sat down at the kitchen table where everyone always congregated.

Eve would have argued how nice she was. She felt she'd let down her family because from the time she was very young, she knew she was different and resented it, always searching for her real self. Her real family, as she thought of them. She'd just wanted someone who looked like her. Now she had Bridger, at least.

"Any luck?" Bridger asked picking up one of the papers spread out on the kitchen table.

"I called all of the Constance Smalls I've found so far," Eve said pouring him a cup of coffee before sitting down at the table with him. Later she would try the C. Small listings.

"You realize she probably married and changed her name. Her name might not even have been Constance Small. She could have lied about that, given she was a runaway."

"I know." Eve could hear Bridger's reservations. Once they'd found out that Constance Small was probably a runaway, he seemed to back off in the search.

She couldn't blame him. It did feel hopeless. Even if Eve lucked out and found the woman, she'd probably wish she hadn't.

"So? Did Laci have her baby?" she asked, changing the subject.

Bridger's expression quickly shifted from a frown to a broad smile. "She sure did. Jack Bridger Duvall."

"Laci beat her sister and got the name Jack?" Eve laughed. The two sisters had both wanted the name Jack from the time they'd found out they were both carrying boys. They'd agreed that whoever gave birth first got the name.

"Laney went with Jake," Bridger said with a shake of his head. *"Sisters."*

Eve smiled. "I know you brought photographs. Come on, let's see 'em."

"I thought you'd never ask," he said pulling his chair closer to her as he dug out his digital camera.

Eve pushed away the papers with the names of the women who could possibly have given birth to her and her brother, wishing she was more like Bridger. He'd moved on. Why couldn't she?

Chapter Three

"Excuse me, can you tell me who that woman is?" Jud Corbett asked the elderly woman standing next to him. "The one in red."

The Old Town Whitehorse Community Center was packed tonight, the country-western band made up of old-timers who cranked out songs that took Jud back to his youth in Texas.

A smile curled the elderly woman's lips as she glanced across the dance floor, then up at him. "They're the Bailey girls—Eve, Faith and McKenna. Faith is the one in red. Pretty, isn't she?"

"Very," Jud said. "Faith Bailey, huh?" He liked the sound of her name.

The woman beside him cut her eyes to him, her smile knowing. "So why don't you ask her to dance?"

He chuckled. Dancing with him would be the last thing Faith Bailey wanted to do. "That's a good idea."

"Yes, it was in my day, too," the elderly woman said sagely.

Jud moved across the worn wooden dance floor toward Faith, who was flanked on each side by her sisters. After dinner tonight, he'd opted not to stay at the ranch but drive back to his trailer on location to be ready for an early shoot in the morning. At least that had been his excuse to escape the tension at the ranch.

As he was driving through Old Town Whitehorse, he'd seen all the rigs parked around the community center. Slowing, he'd heard the old-time country band. He'd bet himself that the band members wouldn't be a day under seventy—and that his trick-riding cowgirl would be there.

He'd parked and walked back to the community center to find he'd been right on both counts.

As he crossed the dance floor toward Faith Bailey now, he realized she'd already seen him and was trying to look anywhere but at him. Clearly, if she'd had somewhere to run in the crowd of people, she would have.

"Hello again," he said, tipping his Stetson as he stopped directly in front of her.

Seeing that she was trapped, her blue eyes flashed like hot flames. "I'm sorry. Do I know you?"

"I would have sworn we'd crossed paths before," he said and grinned. It had bothered him why she'd been practicing her stunts so far away from her ranch house.

But from the imploring look she was giving him now, he'd wager that she hadn't wanted anyone to see her doing the stunts. Was it possible that not even her sisters knew?

"I guess I could be wrong," he said in a slow Southern drawl. "Why don't we dance and see if we can sort it out? Unless you'd like to discuss it here," he added quickly when he saw she was about to decline.

Her cheeks flushed with heat, those big blue eyes hurling daggers at him. "If you insist."

"I do." He took her hand and drew her to him.

The band had broken into a cowboy jitterbug. He swung her away from her sisters and deeper into the other dancers on the floor.

She was a good dancer, staying with him, matching any move he made even though anger still blazed in her eyes. She apparently didn't like being blackmailed into dancing with him. Talking over the band was out of the question, which was fine since he was enjoying dancing with her and had a bad feeling where their conversation would go.

He swung her around, catching her around her slim waist, their gazes meeting, hers challenging. He liked everything about her, from the fire in her eyes to the arrogant tilt of her chin and the easy, confident way she moved. Faith Bailey was apparently just as home on a dance floor as she was on a horse.

And she wasn't about to let him get the better of her.

He smiled, thoroughly enjoying himself. He was sorry when the song ended and she started to pull away. He drew her back as the band went right into a slow dance.

"So, Faith Bailey," Jud said as he pulled her close, breathing the words at her ear. "Why is it you don't want anyone to know about your trick riding?"

She tensed in his arms. Drawing back slowly, her gaze a furious slit, she said, "Blackmail will only get you so far, Mr. Corbett."

He chuckled. "Come on, why the secrecy? You're good. Damned good. Why hide your talent?"

"We're not all like you, Mr. Corbett," she said. "Some of us have no need to be in the spotlight."

"Jud. Mr. Corbett is my father." His grin broadened. "And you and I are more alike than you think. I recognized myself in you the moment I saw you riding across the prairie. You *love* trick riding, and don't tell me you don't like an audience after that stunt you pulled earlier today. So what are you afraid of?"

"Nothing," she said too quickly, and he knew he'd hit a

nerve. The song ended. "Thank you for the dance." She tried to pull free, but he held her a moment longer.

"Don't worry," he whispered, his gaze locked with hers. "I'll keep your secret."

He'd expected relief in her expression. But instead her eyes narrowed, making it clear she didn't like the fact that it was something else they shared.

As he released her and she disappeared into the crowd on the dance floor, all Jud could think about was seeing her again.

FAITH TRIED to still the trembling in her limbs. She went straight to the punch table and downed a glass. Dancing with Jud Corbett had shaken her badly. She feared there was some truth in what he'd said about them being alike.

A man like that could confuse a woman. Not Faith Bailey, who wasn't susceptible to him. But she pitied other women, who she realized could be easily mesmerized by his good looks and easygoing charm.

She shook off those thoughts, reminding herself that she was furious with him for blackmailing her into dancing with him. A man like that, well, he wasn't one she wanted knowing her secret. Not just about the trick riding.

But another secret, one she'd kept hidden from even herself until she'd opened her eyes and seen Jud Corbett leaning over her earlier today.

Faith now feared Jud Corbett knew her most secret desire.

She shivered, feeling exposed and more vulnerable than she'd ever felt. How was it possible that a man she'd only danced with could know her so well?

"I wondered where you had gone off to," McKenna said, joining her. "That was one of the Corbett brothers you just danced with, wasn't it?"

Faith thought about feigning ignorance. "Uh-huh." She took another glass of punch and sipped it this time, needing something to do with her hands.

"He is certainly good-looking," McKenna commented.

"I hadn't noticed."

McKenna laughed. "You *have* to be kidding. Are you going to pretend you also didn't notice the way he was looking at you?"

Faith remembered only too well how his gaze had locked with hers as he'd tipped his hat. Time had stretched out interminably as she'd stood at the edge of the dance floor praying he would just go away.

Her heart had been beating so hard it seemed the only sound in the room as he'd pulled her to him and out onto the dance floor. She'd feared everyone was watching and getting the wrong idea. Especially her sisters.

And they had.

"You're mistaken," Faith said, knowing her cheeks were still flushed. "He looks at every woman that way."

"Are you talking about Jud Corbett, the stuntman?" Eve asked, joining them. She helped herself to a glass of punch.

Faith shrugged and glanced across the room to where Jud Corbett was standing, his gaze on her. She quickly averted her eyes, feeling her cheeks warm even further.

"I heard Jud Corbett is fearless when it comes to stunts," McKenna said.

"He sounds dangerous," Eve said, and Faith could feel her sister's gaze on her.

"Dangerous" described Jud Corbett perfectly, Faith thought, as she saw the look Jud Corbett gave her as he left the dance.

AFTER THE DANCE, Eve Bailey Jackson got on the phone again. Carter was working late tonight at the sheriff's department—some annual report or something or other.

"I don't like you staying home alone so much," Carter had said earlier. His gaze said he knew about the list of phone numbers, knew the long hours she'd spent gathering them—and calling trying to find her birth mother.

He'd seemed about to say something else but changed his mind. Eve knew he worried that she'd never quit looking for her birth mother and that her unfulfilling quest would sour her and their life together. Or worse, that she'd find her mother and be even more disappointed.

Eve had gone through the long list of C. Small numbers, each time telling herself that this would be the call that would end it.

Now as she started to dial yet another, she felt her heart pound with anticipation and fear. This was the last number on the list.

If this number was another dead end, then it was a sign, she told herself. Her fingers shook as she tapped in each number, a silent prayer on her lips and tears in her eyes as she promised herself this would be the last of it. Her search would end here.

Like her brother, she would move on. Carter wanted to have children. He wanted the two of them to get on with their lives.

She made a solemn promise to herself as the phone at the other end of the line began to ring. She'd run out of options and couldn't bear any more dead ends. She would give up her search for the mother who'd given her and Bridger away. This had to stop.

"No more," she said under her breath as the phone rang once, twice, three times and then, just when Eve was about to hang up, give up for good, a female voice answered.

"Hello?"

Eve had to clear her throat. "Is this Mrs. Small?"

"Yes?"

"My name is Eve Bailey Jackson. I'm trying to locate a Constance Small who lived near Whitehorse, Montana, thirty-four years ago."

"Constance?" the woman repeated. The line went dead.

As hard as she tried to hold them back, Eve felt the tears flow down her cheeks. Another dead end. Her last.

THE CALL CAME out of the blue. Mary Ellen was in the middle of baking cookies for the church fund-raiser. Quickly dusting the flour from her hands, she answered the phone with a cheerful, "Hello."

"Mary Ellen?"

"What's wrong, Mother?"

"I got another one of those calls about Constance." Her mother was crying. "After all these years... I just can't bear it. I know it's just another prank call, someone wanting money, like the others professing to have information about Constance."

"It's all right, Mother." But Mary Ellen feared it wasn't. As she'd said, it had been years. Why would someone be calling now?

"I took down the woman's number from caller ID. She said her name was Eve Bailey Jackson. She was calling from Montana."

Mary Ellen drew up a chair and sat down hard.

"She sounded nice." Her mother thought everyone was nice. "But I just can't do it. Would you call her?" Her mother began to cry, and Mary Ellen hated this Eve Bailey Jackson.

"I'll take care of it. I'm sure it's just as you say—nothing. So don't worry yourself over it."

For years Mary Ellen had feared this day would come. But as time had gone by, she'd started to think that the truth would never come out.

"Bless you, dear. Here's her phone number."

Mary Ellen listened as her mother rattled off the Whitehorse, Montana, telephone number, but she didn't write it down. She had no intention of returning the call. She told herself she was doing them all a favor as she hung up the phone.

Turning back toward the kitchen, she saw black smoke billowing from the oven. She'd burned the cookies for the church fund-raiser. Only then did she let herself break down.

Chapter Four

The prairie glistened in the morning sun, tall green grasses undulating in the slight breeze, the smell of summer sharp and sweet. Overhead, puffy white clouds floated in a crystalline blue sky.

Faith saw the plume of dust curling up off the dirt road that ran through Old Town Whitehorse past the Bailey Ranch.

She watched as the vehicle slowed, squinting into the morning sun as a vaguely familiar pickup pulled to a stop in front of the house.

"Is that Jud Corbett?" Eve asked from behind her as the cowboy climbed out of the truck. Tilting his Stetson back, he walked toward the front door.

Faith cursed under her breath. Jud Corbett hadn't taken her warning to stay away. The man was impossible. What could he want? Not to help protect her secrets, she'd bet money on that.

Faith hurried out on the porch and down the steps to cut him off. He was tall and muscled, but there was grace and fluidity to his movements. She easily recognized him in the movies where he did the stunts. There was just something about him. A confidence.

Arrogance, she thought now.

He saw her and slowed as if only now thinking twice about coming here. His mistake.

"I thought we had an understanding?" she demanded through gritted teeth as she faced him.

He grinned then, his eyes sparkling with humor. "Did we?" He took a step toward her. She took two back. "Do I scare you?"

"Of course not," she snapped, a clear lie. What was it about him that made her feel she always had to be on guard around him? She knew the answer to that one, actually.

"Fearless, are you? Then you're just the woman I'm looking for."

She irritably brushed away his words like a cobweb in her path. "Do not even try to charm me. I can assure you it won't work." Another lie.

"That wasn't charm. That was honesty." He said the words simply, and if she hadn't known better, she might have believed him. "I need to talk to you about something that will make you very happy."

She eyed him suspiciously. "If this is about *breakfast*—"

He laughed. "While I would hope *breakfast* with me would make you more than *very* happy, that's not it." The grin faded. "Could we talk somewhere?"

Eve was just inside, probably watching them from the window.

"Down by the creek," Faith said, and turned toward the copse of cottonwoods that stood along the banks. She planned to set the man straight once and for all. The last thing she needed was him showing up on her doorstep again.

While he'd promised to keep her secret, she knew given the way he'd blackmailed her into dancing with him last night that he couldn't be trusted. What was he doing here? And what could he possibly have to talk to her about?

Whatever it was, she was on her guard. She wouldn't put anything past him.

When they reached the creek and were out of sight of the house, she turned to face him, hands on hips, her expression as impatient as she could make it.

"This had better be good," she warned him.

"Our stunt double was bitten by a rattlesnake this morning. She isn't going to be able to finish the shoot."

"Brooke Keith?" Faith said on a surprised breath. She'd heard that the stuntwoman was working on the film. An old flame of Jud's, according to the tabloid movie magazines.

He raised a brow. "You *know* her?"

"Know *of* her. I've read about her." The moment those words were out, Faith wanted to snatch them back.

Jud's brows shot up. "So that's it. You don't really believe that stuff Hollywood gossip rags print, do you?" He shook his head as if disappointed in her.

"Where there's smoke, there is usually fire," she said, grimacing at how much she sounded like her sister Eve.

"Look, I'd like to try to convince you that you're all wrong about me, but I don't have the time," Jud said. "We need someone to fill in for Brooke and finish the film. There are only a few more days of stunts to be shot. I suggested you to our director."

He rushed on. "The director checked and found out that you already have a SAG card." His gaze narrowed. "Apparently you've done some ride-on parts in movies, not stunts, just horse-related shots—this woman who shuns the spotlight."

He held up his hand to stop her from commenting. It was a wasted effort on his part. She'd opened her mouth, but nothing had come out. A small gust of wind could have knocked her over.

Jud Corbett hadn't just known her secret heart's desire—he'd just offered it to her.

"If you pass this up," he said. "You'll regret it the rest of your life."

"I…"

"Just think about it." He thrust a business card into her hand. "My cell phone number's on it. I'll just need to know by noon." With that he turned and walked away, leaving her too stunned to move.

DIRECTOR ERIK ZANDER couldn't believe his bad luck. Just the thought made him curse as he poured Scotch into his fourth cup of coffee of the morning. Probably wasn't the best way to start the day, but what the hell, given the way his life was going.

Last night Keyes Hasting had called.

"I heard about the film you're making and am intrigued," Hasting said. "You don't mind if I come up."

Like hell he didn't mind, but he'd been too shocked to say so, especially when Hasting had added, "The theme of this film is close to my heart. Retribution, isn't it?"

Those last words registered like a gun to his head.

"I heard your stuntwoman was bitten by a rattlesnake," Hasting had said. "I hope you can find someone else so you can finish the film."

"My stunt coordinator has someone in mind," he'd said, all the time thinking, *That son of a bitch Hasting has a spy on the set.*

Hasting was an old reprobate with too much money and alleged mob connections. Zander had hung up the phone and gotten skunk drunk. And this morning, hungover, he was dreading Hasting's visit like a root canal.

Snapping open his cell phone, Zander checked to see if

Jud had called. No voice mail. Jud had promised to let him know the moment he had a verbal agreement from the new stuntwoman. Why hadn't he heard something yet?

Fortunately, he would be able to shoot around the problem today, but by tomorrow when Hasting arrived...

"Anyone seen Jud Corbett?" Zander bellowed as he stepped out of his trailer, wishing he'd never laid eyes on the script for this film. It had arrived on his doorstep. Along with a blackmail threat.

FAITH WAS STILL standing by the creek when Jud Corbett drove away in his pickup. He had her stirred up good, and no matter how hard she tried to put him—and his offer— out of her mind, she couldn't.

She'd always dreamed of being a stuntwoman, specializing like many did with horse trick riding.

But it had only been a dream. She'd told herself her riding gave her so much pleasure, she didn't need to take it any further. Only men like Jud Corbett needed the applause and exaltation.

But he'd called her on it and now the truth was out. She wanted this more than she'd ever wanted anything, she thought, as she walked back toward the house. She'd just never admitted it. Until now.

Faith looked up to see her sister waiting on the porch for her, a worried look on her face. Faith swallowed and said, "There's something I need to tell you."

As she took a seat beside Eve, she spilled it all, the years of practice and Jud Corbett's offer—her most secret of all desires.

"I wondered how long it would take you to tell me," Eve said when Faith had finished.

"You *knew?*"

"Oh, Faith, I've known since that time when you were a girl and you broke your arm. I'd hoped you would outgrow it. I was afraid for you. But when you didn't... It's what you've always wanted, isn't it?"

She nodded, tears in her eyes. "When we were kids, I thought you'd tell Mother, then after I went away to college, I just didn't want to worry you."

"You've been headed in this direction for a long time."

Just as Jud had said, in college Faith had done some ride-on parts in movies being filmed around Bozeman. None involved stunts, though.

"Don't think it doesn't worry me," her sister continued. "Stunt work is dangerous."

"It can be," Faith allowed. "You have to use your head, expect things to go wrong. It's all part of it."

Eve shook her head. "McKenna will probably have a fit, not to mention what Mother will have to say about it. But Dad, well, he'll just be proud of you."

Faith smiled. If she had expected anyone to have a fit, it was Eve. Life was just full of surprises. She hugged her older sister. "Thank you. I have to call Jud and tell him I'll do it."

"You hadn't already agreed?" Eve asked in surprise.

"I wanted to talk to you first."

Tears welled in her sister's eyes. "I would never stand in your way. But just so you know, I intend to be on that set every day you're doing a stunt."

Faith laughed and went to make the call. Jud answered on the first ring as if he'd been waiting for her call.

"So you're going to do it," he said before she could say a word. He sounded pleased, an underlying excitement in his voice that tripped something inside her.

"You're that sure I can do this?" she had to ask.

He chuckled. "You know you can or you wouldn't have called me back."

"Don't be so sure about that."

"We resume shooting in the morning, but come over this afternoon. I've made sure there will be a trailer here for you to stay in so you'll be ready for early shoots. Bring your horse. There will be time to get in some riding."

He had everything arranged already? "What if I hadn't called?"

"I saw you ride, remember? You and I are cut from the same cloth."

"Except I will never be as cocky as you are."

He laughed. "Trust me, you already are." She could tell he was smiling. "This is a great break for you. I'm as excited about it as I was when I did my first film."

Faith swallowed, thinking that her break had come at the expense of the stuntwoman who'd been bitten by a rattlesnake and said as much.

"Brooke's going to be fine. The doctor said she's one of those rare cases. She had an adverse reaction to the snakebite antidote. Fortunately, we have a helicopter on the set and rushed her to the hospital."

"Once she gets better, she'll want her job back," Faith said, worried that was true.

"Nope. You'll be doing what's left of her stunt work for the remainder of the shoot. She talked the director into hiring her as assistant stunt coordinator. She can't do stunts, but she can help set them up."

Faith swallowed back her guilt at that news. She couldn't help but be anxious and thrilled at the same time. Jud had seen to everything. "Are you always so accommodating?" she asked only half-joking.

"I made an exception just for you. I should warn you,"

he added, "this film is pretty low budget. As well as doing stunts, I'm also the stunt director. But don't worry. I think you'll be pleased with what I got you for pay."

As if she wouldn't have done it for free, Faith thought.

"Celebrate," Jud said.

Again she felt that small insistent thrill that seemed to warm her blood. "Jud?"

"Yes?"

"Thank you."

He laughed. "Thank me after this film is over. This will either cure you of your need to trick ride or—"

"Or kill me?" she asked with a nervous laugh.

"Or hook you so badly you won't want to ever quit," he said. "Either way, you may not thank me when it's over."

She wondered about that as she hung up and felt like pinching herself. Her secret desire was about to be realized. She just had to be careful that Jud Corbett didn't ignite any other secret desires in her.

As she started to leave, she noticed some wadded-up papers in the wastebasket near the phone. She pulled one out and saw that it was the list of numbers for Constance Small and C. Small. Every name had been scratched out.

Dropping the paper back into the trash, she glanced toward the porch where Eve was still sitting and felt an overwhelming sadness for her sister. If only her dreams could come true.

MARY ELLEN HATED FLYING. She'd brought along some needlepoint for the flight, but she hadn't touched it. Her mind was reeling. What did she hope to accomplish by flying to Montana? Just the thought of returning to Whitehorse made her blood run cold.

Had she been able, she would have gotten off the plane

and gone home where she belonged. But as she felt the plane begin its descent into Billings, Mary Ellen knew she'd come too far to turn back now. She had to see why after all these years someone would call about Constance.

There would be a rental car waiting for her at the airport on the rock rims above Montana's largest city, but she was arriving so late that she planned to spend the night and drive the three hours to Whitehorse in the morning.

From Billings she could drive north through Roundup and Grass Range, the only two towns for hundreds of miles between Billings and Whitehorse. Roundup was small, and Grass Range was even smaller.

Mary Ellen tightened her seat belt and closed her eyes. She hated cold even more than flying. At least it was July in Montana. Had it been winter like the last time she was in Whitehorse, Mary Ellen knew she wouldn't have come.

It would be hard enough returning to the past.

As the plane began its descent into Billings, Mary Ellen wished she were on speaking terms with God. But she suspected any prayers from her would be futile given all her sins—her greatest sin committed in Whitehorse, Montana, thirty-four years ago.

As FAITH TOPPED THE HILL in her pickup, her horse trailer towed behind, she saw the movie encampment below: the two circles of trailers and past it the small town that had been erected. All of it had a surreal feel to it—not unlike this opportunity that had landed in her lap.

Captured in the dramatic light of the afternoon sun, the small Western town in the middle of the Montana prairie looked almost real with its false storefronts, wooden sidewalks, hitching posts with horses tied to them and people dressed as they would have been a hundred years ago.

She'd barely gotten out of her pickup when Jud Corbett walked up.

"Feel like saddling up and going for a ride?" he asked.

"Sure." She hadn't been on her horse all day, and the offer definitely had its appeal. Even more so because it would be with Jud, although she wasn't about to admit that, even to herself.

They saddled their horses and rode along the edge of the ravine overlooking the movie camp. She and Jud compared childhoods, both finding that they'd grown up on ranches some distance from town, both loved horses and both had begun riding at an early age.

"I can't believe how much we have in common," Jud said, his gaze warming her more than the afternoon summer sun. "Do you believe in fate?"

She chuckled. "Let me guess. It's *fate* that you and I met?"

"Don't you think so?" he asked. He was grinning, but she saw that he was also serious.

"I suppose I do." If he hadn't taken the back road to his family ranch that evening, and if Laney and Laci hadn't gone into labor when they had so Faith could go riding, then what was the chance that she and Jud would be here right now?

"Fate, whatever, I'm just glad you and I crossed paths," he said, then drew up his horse, as below them the ghost town came into view.

Jud leaned on his saddle horn to stare down at it. "Spooky looking, even from here."

She felt a chill as she followed his gaze. A tumbleweed cartwheeled slowly down the main street of the ghost town to come to rest with a pile of others against the side of one of the buildings. Remarkable there were any buildings still standing.

"So are the stories true?" Jud asked.

"At least some of them," she said. "The descendants of the Brannigan family still live on down the river." She saw his surprise. "Some of the descendants of Kid Curry and his brothers also still live around here."

He shook his head. "But what about the town and this thing with the rag dolls?"

She looked down at what was left of Lost Creek. "I'm sure you've heard the story, since apparently it's what the script of this film is based on."

"Some outlaws rode into town and killed a woman and her little girl while the townspeople stood by and did nothing. The husband and eldest son returned, saw his dead wife and child in the middle of the street and picking up the little girl's rag doll from the street, swore vengeance on everyone who'd stood back and let it happen. Does that about size it up?"

She smiled. "Just about."

"Then the townspeople started finding rag dolls on their doorstep and terrible things began to happen to them until one night everyone in town disappeared."

"That's the way the story goes," Faith admitted.

"Don't you think its more than likely the townspeople left knowing that the outlaws would be back and more of them would die?" Jud asked.

She said nothing.

"What happened to the father?"

"Orville Brannigan and the rest of his children moved downriver to live like hermits. Their descendants still do. The little girl's gravestone is about all that's left up at the cemetery on the hill. Emily Brannigan. The historical society comes out a couple of times a year and puts flowers on her grave."

"The poor family," Jud said.

"It always amazes me how many families struggled to tame this land and still do."

"Like *your* family."

She nodded, remembering the school field trip she'd taken to the Lost Creek ghost town and the frightening sensation that had come over as she'd stood among the old buildings on the dirt street where Emily Brannigan and her mother had lost their lives.

That sensation had been the presence of evil. Evil fueled by vengeance. She'd known then that the settlers had never left town. Some years back, a local named Bud Lynch had sworn he found a pile of human bones in a cave west of the ghost town.

The bones, as well as any evidence of the more than hundred-year-old crime, had mysteriously disappeared before his story could be confirmed by the sheriff.

The Brannigans and their relatives called Bud Lynch a liar, but Faith had seen the man's face when he told of what had to have been the skeletons of dozens of men, women and children, piled like kindling in the bottom of the cave.

There was no doubt that Bud Lynch had seen evil.

DIRECTOR ERIK ZANDER WOKE on the couch, confused for a moment where he was and how he'd gotten there. On the floor next to him lay an overturned empty Scotch bottle. He groaned when he saw it.

He had to quit drinking like this. He sat up, his head aching, the room spinning for a moment. The trailer rocked to the howl of the wind outside, the motion making him ill.

He glanced at his watch. Past two in the morning. With an early call, he really needed to get some sleep. Hasting would be arriving today, and who knew what the hell he really wanted.

Pushing himself to his feet, Zander stumbled toward the bedroom, slowing as he passed the kitchen and the fresh bottle of Scotch he knew was in the cabinet within reach.

"Don't even think about it," he mumbled to himself. He was already so drunk he had trouble navigating the narrow hallway, bumping from wall to wall like a pinball. Something about that made him laugh.

He was still chuckling when he reached the small bedroom. The trailer room was just large enough for a bed and a built-in dresser.

As he aimed himself for the bed, he spotted the doll propped against the pillow and lurched back, stumbling into the wall and sitting down hard. Now eye to eye with the damned doll, he saw that it had to be the ugliest thing he'd ever seen.

Worse, it appeared to be looking right at him, reminding him how much he hated this script. A Western *thriller?* As if his life couldn't get any worse.

He reached for the doll, squeezing it in his big hand as he stared into its grotesque face. It wasn't until then that it registered in his alcohol-saturated brain that it wasn't one of the dolls from props.

He stumbled to his feet, still clutching the doll. "What the hell is this?" If it wasn't from props, then where had it come from? And why had someone left it on his bed?

At least that answer was easier to come up with. Anyone who'd read the script knew that the rag dolls were the harbinger of bad luck and had made it thinking to scare him.

Erik Zander began to laugh, a big belly laugh that sent him sprawling backward on the bed. As if some ugly doll could make his life any worse.

Chapter Five

"It's a *ruse*," Nancy told Zander the next morning. She'd come straight to his trailer before the others were even up.

The director had stumbled to the door, still half-asleep, wearing blue cotton pajama bottoms. His graying blond hair stuck out at all angles, and there was a red crease line on his unshaven jaw where he'd slept on something that had left a mark.

Although in his early fifties, he still looked like the boy next door—the drop-dead good-looking boy who never gave a second glance to nondescript girls like Nancy Davis.

She couldn't help but stare at his muscular bare chest. It was covered with blond-gray fuzz that fell in a V to the tied pj bottoms. Even at this age, he was still a damned good-looking man. She felt her face heat and hurriedly averted her eyes.

"I have to talk to you," she stammered.

"What the hell time is it?"

"I came by before anyone else was up so we wouldn't be interrupted."

He grunted. "Well, come in then." After a hasty retreat to the back of the trailer, he returned wearing a faded and worn publicity T-shirt from his last movie over the pajama bottoms.

"I'm sorry to wake you so early, but I knew you'd want to know," Nancy said. "It's about Chantal and Nevada."

He held up a hand as he got the coffee going. "It's too damned early to even talk about them, okay?"

"They're only pretending to hate each other," she blurted. "I saw them together last night."

"The moment will pass, believe me. Like the quiet before the storm." He hovered over the coffeemaker as if intimidation could force it to brew faster. "Don't you know? They do this all the time."

"I've seen their fights on YouTube. I didn't buy it then and I certainly don't now. They're deceiving everyone."

He turned to frown in her direction. "*Okay.* Who cares?"

Nancy was surprised by his lack of interest. Was the man daft?

"Believe me, by this morning they'll be at each other's throats again and trying to destroy this film," he said with a sigh as he lifted the coffeepot and motioned in her direction.

"No, thanks," she said and watched him pour himself a cup. He turned his back to her to add a shot of Scotch to the coffee, as if everyone didn't know about his drinking.

"It just seems strange that they'd want everyone on the set to think they hate each other. I mean, they've hung their dirty laundry out for everyone to see for months now. Why the secrecy? It has to be a publicity stunt to keep their photos on the front of every tabloid out there."

Zander scowled as he took a gulp of his coffee and leaned back into the kitchen counter as if he needed the support. "When I think of the heated battles they've put us all through on the set…" He shook his head and took another gulp of coffee. "But quite frankly, I could give a damn what they do as long as they don't destroy this film, and this morning I'm not even sure I care about that."

She gave him a disapproving look. "Well, I just thought you should know since I'm aware how much this film means to your career."

"Yeah," he said and took another gulp of coffee and Scotch.

She rose and walked to the door, turning to look back at him.

He was squinting down into this coffee cup. He'd completely forgotten she was there.

Nancy wondered what would happen if he ever really took a good look at her. One thing was certain. It wasn't going to happen today.

THE SET WAS A BEEHIVE of activity the next morning when Faith came out of her trailer. She'd been on other location shoots and knew that filmmaking was a lot of standing around and waiting. It was never as exciting as she'd originally thought it would be.

But today was completely different. She couldn't have been more excited. Jud was waiting for her at catering, a bunch of tables and chairs under a tent with a trailer next to it. The set was too far away from anything to be catered, so cooks had been hired to feed everyone.

He handed her a cup of coffee, smiling broadly.

"How's the nerves?" he asked.

"Steady as a rock."

He laughed. "I'll bet. Have some coffee and then I'll fill you in on what's planned for today. Once we get your paperwork taken care of, next stop is makeup and wardrobe."

Since she would be standing in for the leading lady, Faith was going to be dressed identically to what Chantal would be wearing today. Her blond hair was close enough in color to the star's that at least she wouldn't have to wear a wig—just a large bonnet, which would hide most of her hair anyway.

"I feel as if I've stepped back a hundred years," Faith said later as she came out of the costume trailer to find Jud waiting for her. She was wearing a prairie dress, lace-up high-heeled boots, her hair drawn up under the bonnet.

His gaze was hotter than the sun peeking over the horizon. "Wow. You look…"

She couldn't imagine him being at a loss for words.

"Perfect," he said finally and laughed.

They walked to a waiting SUV that drove them to the temporary set. A facade of a town had been erected to resemble what Lost Creek would have looked like over a hundred years ago.

The storefronts appeared real enough, but behind each was nothing but supports or, in the case of the hotel, a building that housed a saloon with a staircase up to the second floor where there was a hallway and one room that looked out over the main street.

Horses were already tied to the hitching posts and several wagons were parked along the street. Crew worked to move props and camera equipment into place. The cast and crew were smaller than some of the films she'd worked on, which made it feel more intimate. Or maybe it was just being this close to Jud Corbett.

"That's our leading lady," Jud said, as Chantal Lee came out of the saloon and stopped on the wooden sidewalk. She appeared irritated as she dusted at something on her sleeve. From a distance, she could have been Faith's twin.

"And our leading man, Nevada Wells." Nevada stood in the swinging doors at the front of the saloon as if posing for his picture. But no one was paying any attention to him. He, however, had his gaze on Chantal.

Faith recognized them both from films and the tabloids and movie magazines.

Jud walked Faith through the stunts they would be performing. He would be doing Nevada's stunts and stand-ins, she Chantal's.

He pointed to a wagon pulled by a team of horses. "Have you ever driven a team before? It's not that hard since the object is to let them run so the hero, that would be me, can chase you down and save you. Of course they don't run as fast and as out of control as they will appear on film."

Faith smiled at him, thinking this was a lot like her fantasies as a girl on the ranch. Only in those, she did the saving.

"I'm a quick study," she said as they walked over to the wagon and she climbed up on the seat.

"We're going to do a few slow-motion run-throughs, then the main event later. You ready?"

Faith grinned. She couldn't wait.

THE RUNAWAY WAGON was a stunt straight out of old Westerns. On a higher budget film, most of the action would have been computer generated.

"I want this film as authentic as we can make it," Zander had said to Jud. "None of that computer-generated stuff."

Jud had only nodded, although he knew the director was just being cheap. Computer-generated material was costly. And even though Zander would have to pay Jud more for the dangerous stunts, he would still save money. Stunt money hadn't been as good the last few years because a lot of films had gone with computer-generated action scenes.

Not that Jud worried about making more money. He didn't do this for the money. He liked to do the stunts. The runaway wagon stunt could be dangerous. Driving a team of horses wasn't as easy as it looked. Not that he was worried that Faith couldn't handle it.

But there had already been a few minor accidents on the film. Not unusual in the filmmaking industry, but he just wanted to be sure that Faith was as safe as possible since he'd gotten her into this.

He climbed up onto the wagon seat next to her and unhooked the reins. "Let's take a little ride first to let you get the feel of it."

They took off down the dirt track. They hadn't gone far when she took the reins. At the foothills, she turned the team around.

"Let's try it with some speed," she said with a grin and snapped the reins down. The team took off, gaining speed as they raced back toward the fabricated town.

Faith slowed the wagon on the outskirts of the set and brought the team to a halt. "Well?"

Jud grinned over at her. This woman could handle anything she set her mind to. "The idea is to let them run, but not too fast."

She nodded. "I know. It's all illusion." The team wouldn't actually be out of control. The wagon seat was rigged so it rocked. All Faith had to do was play along.

"You got it." Jud jumped down and lifted her from the wagon. Her waist was slim, her body warm beneath the dress. He set her down and for a moment he had this wild desire to kiss her.

She must have sensed it because she stepped away from him.

At the sound of raised voices he turned to see Chantal arguing with the director.

"You don't need me at all today," Chantal was saying, even though she was down on the call sheet for the first scene, where she has a discussion with the leading man while sitting on the seat of the wagon.

The runaway wagon scene would follow. Although most scenes were shot out of sequence, the cinematographer had wanted these in order to make sure the light was the same and save filming yet another day since, according to the weatherman, a storm was moving in.

Jud walked over to see what was going on.

"Shoot my double," Chantal said. "I told you, I'm ill. I'm going to my trailer." Without another word she stormed over to one of the trucks used to ferry crew and actors from the encampment to the set and took off.

Zander swore and turned to Jud. "We'll shoot around her." It was becoming the film's mantra.

Jud glanced toward Faith, who must have overheard. She gave him a thumbs-up and climbed back onto the wagon bench.

Jud headed for his horse, motioning to the cinematographer and director that they were ready.

The scene would be shot from several angles. This scene required that Faith as Chantal's body double race across the prairie on the runaway wagon after a fictional gunshot from the saloon spooked her team.

As he started to swing into the saddle, Jud caught movement out of the corner of his eye. Something flew past. The rest happened so quickly, all he could do was react.

One of the horses in the team started for no apparent reason, rearing up, then taking off. Jud saw Faith grab for the reins from where she was sitting on the wagon's seat as the horses panicked and bolted.

Jud leaped on his horse and went racing after her. He could see the film crew scrambling to get out of the way as the wagon careened toward them.

Faith's bonnet blew off, her long blond hair coming loose and blowing back in a wave. She was struggling to get control of the team—and to still stay on the wagon as it rattled across the rough terrain.

Jud rode hard after her. The wagon hit a bump and Faith went airborne for a moment before coming down again half on the seat. She regained her balance but lost one of the reins. The team ran flat out, even more spooked with one of the reins dragging now.

Gaining on the wagon, Jud rode up along the right side. He'd performed this stunt a dozen times—just not at this speed. Nor out in the middle of the prairie without a fail-safe.

"Faith!"

She nodded and slid across the wagon seat toward him. Her blue eyes were wide with fear, but she did as she would have in the actual scene—only at a much faster speed and through the bumpy prairie.

Ahead he could see an outcropping of rocks. The team of horses was headed right for it. Jud knew he'd get only one chance to do this before the team and wagon reached the rocks.

He reached for Faith.

CHANTAL LEE WATCHED the whole thing from in front of her trailer. She would have assumed that Zander had moved up the stunt. Except there were no cameras rolling.

With horror, she realized that the team of horses had run away for real. This was no movie stunt. And if she hadn't refused to shoot that part today, she would have been on that wagon.

She covered her mouth with her hand as she watched the scene unfold. Just like in the movies—Jud riding to save the cowgirl.

Only this was real.

Chantal heard others join her, a crowd forming around her and cries of horror as Jud reached for the new stunt-woman—an amateur who was about to get killed.

"He's got her!" someone cried.

Chantal blinked, not believing what she'd just seen. The new stuntwoman—what was her name? She'd been told her name this morning, but she hadn't been paying attention. Anyway, she'd made the jump to the back of Jud's horse just before the team veered away from the pile of rocks.

The wagon didn't make the ninety-degree turn, and flipped over, crashing into the rocks, boards splintering and wheels flying as the fail-safe mechanism released the team from the wagon. The team slowed and finally stopped.

Chantal stared at the carnage. "I could have been on that wagon. I was *supposed* to be on that wagon." She glanced across the camp and saw Brooke Keith give her a short nod, a smile on the stuntwoman's face.

Chantal shuddered as she remembered the rag doll she'd found on her bed. Brooke had sworn she hadn't done it. But what if she had? What if it hadn't been a prank, but a warning?

"If you'd been on that wagon, you'd be dead right now," one of the crew said.

"He's right," another said. "If that stuntwoman hadn't known what to do, she'd be in those rocks with her head split open."

"Good thing you were too sick to work," Nancy Davis said.

Chantal hadn't seen the assistant director join them. She heard Nancy's snide tone, but ignored it as Brooke joined them.

"Jud's the one who saved the day, again," Chantal said for Brooke's benefit. "He's the one who killed the rattle-snake that bit you. What would we do without him?"

"Come on, everyone. Let's get back to work," Nancy ordered, shooting a look at Chantal, which she ignored.

The moment everyone else left, Brooke grabbed her arm. "Leave Jud alone, Chantal. I'm warning you."

Chantal jerked her arm free. "You left me that doll."

"It was just a joke."

"Just like that runaway team of horses?"

Brooke shook her head. "I had nothing to do with that. It was just an *accident*."

"Like your snakebite," Chantal said.

As FAITH SLIPPED OFF the back of the horse, Jud swung down and pulled her to him. She wasn't sure her legs would have held her without his strong arms around her. She looked up into his handsome face, never so glad to see anyone in her whole life.

He held her longer than necessary, but she was glad of it. He seemed to be as relieved as she was.

When he finally let her go, she could see the fear still in his eyes. "You're sure you're all right?"

She nodded. "I thought I was a goner." She was safe, standing on solid ground. So why did being this close to Jud make her feel as if the earth might crumble under her at any moment?

"Did you see what spooked the horses?" he asked.

She shook her head. "There was a thunk, as if a rock hit the side of the wagon," she said, frowning as she tried to remember. "It happened so fast, I can't be sure."

"A rock. Did you see where it came from?"

She thought it an odd question. "No." Was he saying he thought someone might have thrown the rock? And why was he acting as if this wasn't the first accident on the set?

Whatever it had been, the scene was straight out of the

movies, with Jud saving her. The realization of just how close a call it had been was starting to settle in. She hugged herself to still the trembling. "You saved my life. Thank you."

He looked ill at ease. "I was just doing my job."

"Too bad they didn't get it on film," she said, making him smile. She could see that he was upset.

"You did great."

"I just did what you showed me to do." That, and she'd studied enough of the stunts on old movies.

He glanced toward the set. One of the SUVs was headed in their direction. He walked over to pick up his horse's reins.

His gaze met hers and held it before they were descended on by the others from the set. "I hope I haven't gotten you into something dangerous," he said quietly.

She frowned as he swung up onto his horse. What did he mean? Of course stunt work was dangerous sometimes.

But she had the feeling he was talking about something else, as if he thought the runaway team hadn't been an accident.

Chapter Six

Jud heard someone come up behind him as he headed for his trailer, but he paid no attention. He was still shaken by what had happened. Faith Bailey was lucky to be alive.

"Saved another one, huh?" said an angry-sounding male voice behind him.

Jud turned to find Nevada Wells, face flushed, eyes bulging, his breathing coming hard and fast. Nevada was Hollywood handsome complete with a cleft in his chin, but apparently just the altitude left the man winded.

"I've got your number," the leading man said, poking a finger into Jud's chest. "If you think I don't know what you're up to, I do. The rest of these people, they're too stupid to see, but not me." His breath smelled of alcohol and he looked as if he hadn't gotten much sleep lately.

"What the hell are you talking about?" Jud asked impatiently. There was nothing about Nevada Wells he liked. The man had gotten this far on looks, not talent, and was known for being a wuss as well as a whiner.

"The snake, now the runaway wagon. Lucky you just happened to be there both times."

"*You* were there, as well," Jud said pointedly, but Nevada clearly wasn't listening.

"You like playing hero."

Jud laughed. "You're the one who *plays* hero."

Nevada narrowed his eyes. "What do you think Erik Zander would say if I told him I know who's behind the accidents on the set?"

"He'd say you were crazy as well as drunk. Don't be ludicrous. What would I have to gain by doing something so malicious?"

"I've been asking myself that."

"Let me know when you come up with an answer," Jud said and walked off.

AFTER A HOT SHOWER and a change into jeans, shirt and boots, Faith left her trailer to find her sister. She had tried Eve's cell phone but had gotten voice mail. Eve hadn't planned to come out to the shoot until afternoon, when Faith had told her she'd be doing her first stunt. A small fib.

Faith suspected her sister had heard about the accident, given the way news traveled in the county. So she wasn't surprised to see Eve among the locals who came out to watch moviemaking from the sidelines.

A rope barrier had been erected to keep back what had been until now only a small crowd. Several crew members were now positioned nearby in case someone tried to get on the set during shooting.

Eve Bailey was standing with some other local residents Faith recognized. From her sister's expression, Faith could see that Eve was upset. No doubt she'd been told that Faith was all right, but Eve would have to see for herself, and the crew wasn't about to let her through to find her sister.

As she drew near, Faith noticed a woman standing off

to the side away from the locals. What caught Faith's attention was the way the woman was dressed. She wore a pale green dress and low heels, her hair pulled up in a chignon.

That alone made her stand out since everyone else was dressed in jeans and boots. While Faith would swear she'd never seen the woman before, something about her seemed familiar. She had wide-set dark eyes and dark hair streaked with gray. She wore a scarf around her neck, tied loosely, that picked up the green in the dress.

Something else odd: she didn't seem that interested in what was happening on the set. Instead, she was looking down the rope line, her gaze on the locals.

Faith worked her way around the back of the small crowd, not wanting to block anyone's view of the scene being shot. When she touched her sister's shoulder, Eve turned and, seeing her, dragged her into a tight hug without a word.

"I'm fine," Faith said as others she knew crowded around her, wanting to hear the gory details. "It was just like the real stunt and worked exactly the same," she said, stretching the truth.

When she looked up, she saw the woman in green watching them. Caught, the woman hurriedly glanced away. When Faith looked again, the woman was headed for an SUV with Billings plates.

"Are you sure you're all right?" Eve asked, drawing Faith's attention back.

Faith nodded, looking into her sister's heart-shaped face framed by her long black hair, the eyes so dark they were almost black, and felt a jolt as she saw the resemblance between the older woman who'd just left in the SUV—and her sister.

MARY ELLEN DROVE to the top of the hill and had to pull over and get herself under control before continuing back to Whitehorse.

At breakfast this morning at the Great Northern, she'd heard the locals talking about the film and Faith Bailey.

The name Bailey had caught her attention. She'd listened as the group of women, who were apparently from some group called the Whitehorse Sewing Circle, discussed an accident on the set this morning. Apparently Eve Bailey was on her way out there, even though early reports were that her younger sister Faith was fine.

"What's that girl doing out there performing stunts anyway?" one of the older women demanded.

"She's a *Bailey*. You know how wild those girls always were," another one said.

"Lila raised them like boys. That was the problem."

"Raised 'em more like wolves, if you ask me." Everyone laughed. "It's no surprise the way that youngest one is turning out."

The women finished their breakfasts and decided to drive out to the set to see just what that youngest Bailey girl was up to before going back to Old Town Whitehorse to finish a couple of baby quilts they were all working on for the Cavanaugh girls.

Mary Ellen had pushed her half-finished breakfast away and followed, hoping they were right about Eve Bailey being on this movie set. What would it hurt to see the woman? she'd thought. She'd come this far.

And she had seen her. Mary Ellen would have recognized Eve anywhere. The dark hair, those coal-black eyes so much like her own and that face. It was like looking into a photograph taken thirty-some years before.

Her heart was still pounding. She felt sick to her

stomach. She wished she'd never come here. Never laid eyes on Eve Bailey Jackson. Never seen the way the sisters had hugged so tightly and realized how much she'd missed the past thirty-four years.

Mary Ellen wiped at her tears and checked her watch. If she hurried back to the motel and packed up she might be able to catch an early flight out.

If she stayed in Whitehorse any longer, she feared what she might do. As she drove away from the movie set, she barely noticed the bank of dark clouds over the Little Rockies.

THE SKY DARKENED to the west, the wind kicking up dust devils as it swept down the river and through the badlands of the Missouri Breaks. A lightning bolt tore through the clouds in the distance, and the rumble of thunder echoed over the set.

Zander cursed. Not even the weather would cooperate. He ran a hand through his hair and scowled at the sky. The whole day had gone this way, beginning with the team of horses taking off the way they had and destroying the wagon.

It was a wonder Faith Bailey hadn't gotten killed. She would have if it hadn't been for Jud Corbett. Hiring him was the best thing Zander had done. Not that it had been his choice. He'd had no choice. And that's what worried him now.

Along with the script and the blackmail note, he'd found instructions on who to cast, what stunt people to use, what crew members. Thinking it was some crackpot, he'd tossed the script and the blackmail note into the garbage.

A day later, when the second blackmail note had arrived with a copy of a very incriminating photograph taken the night of the party at his Malibu beach house—a night that had ended with crime-scene tape and a coroner's van— he'd dug the script out of the garbage and read it.

He'd quickly been convinced that making a Western thriller near Whitehorse, Montana was in his best interests.

Now as he watched the clouds moving fast up the river, he wondered if he'd not only been set up—but also set up to fail. Zander laughed at his own foolishness. Even blackmailed, a part of him believed the person doing this was just someone who was desperate to get his film made.

He'd been able to fool himself—until Keyes Hasting had showed up this morning at his trailer and had mentioned, almost as an offhand remark, that he was in mourning. His godchild, he said, had recently died.

"I'm sorry," Zander had said automatically, since what else was there to say?

"She was a beautiful woman—talented, headstrong and determined, probably too determined, but now we will never know what she might have accomplished in her life," Hasting said.

There was an edge to his voice that should have put Zander on alert. But he was too busy wondering why Hasting had come to pick up on it.

"You knew her."

Zander had been fiddling with the coffeemaker, but at those words, he stopped and turned, frowning slightly. "Your godchild?"

"That was who we were talking about, wasn't it?" the old man snapped irritably.

Zander had finally picked up on that scalpel-edge tone of Hasting's. "*I* knew her?" His heart boomed in his chest. Had it been some young, starry-eyed actress he'd rejected for a film? Or fired? Or far worse, slept with? He had barely heard Hasting's next words because he'd been breathing so hard, his pulse like a barreling freight train.

"You knew her *well. Very* well. Her name was Camille Rush."

Looking back, Zander could now marvel at how well he'd taken the news that this old mob-connected gangster's godchild was the young starlet Zander had impregnated and refused to marry. The same starlet who'd been found in his hot tub dead and full of drugs.

"Keyes," he'd said, actually using the old man's first name. "I'm so sorry. I had no idea Camille was your godchild. I regret that I didn't realize she was in trouble," he'd said in his defense, his voice filled with true emotion—fear, though, more than true remorse. "But how could I know that she would take her own life?"

Hasting had scowled at him, then laughed. "We both know Camille was too self-centered to ever take her own life."

Zander thought of the way the man had then walked away, the threat hanging in the air like the dark clouds now gathering.

That's when he knew for certain. This film. Keyes Hasting was the one behind it and the blackmail. The question that had tormented Zander then and now, though, was still *why?* Some kind of warped revenge? Hasting could have had him killed and been done with it. Why go to all this trouble?

True, the way the film was going, this would be a much slower, more painful death, Zander thought. This film wasn't a lifesaving limb for a drowning man. *Death at Lost Creek* was no doubt the nail in his coffin.

Keyes Hasting planned to destroy his career somehow with this film. Or was there more to it?

One thing was clear. Hasting was his mortal enemy. But what could Zander do? Nothing. Hasting had him right where he wanted him.

Zander shivered, less from the dropping temperature than from his own dark thoughts. Whatever—this day was a wash, literally.

"Strike the set!" he called in disgust and headed toward his trailer. "Reschedule for tomorrow morning, weather permitting," he told his mousy assistant director without giving Nancy a backward glance.

"Erik."

He didn't turn around. In fact, just the sound of Chantal's voice made him want to run as far and fast as he could. He'd already had a run-in with Nevada before breakfast.

His trailer had been like Grand Central Station this morning, starting with Nancy carrying gossip about the stars of the movie, then Nevada with complaints about everything from his accommodations to his role, then Brooke demanding more money since she was now an assistant stunt coordinator.

He felt as if he were on a sinking ship, no life raft and no way to call for help.

After the morning he'd had, he was in no mood to hear Chantal's complaints and demands. He feared he might wring her pretty little neck. If she valued her life, she'd take the hint and leave him alone.

He quickened his step. With luck he would reach his trailer before the rain started and without Chantal. He needed a drink to steady him. He feared the people around him had begun to smell fear coming off him in waves.

"Erik." Chantal's sharp tone cut through his thoughts as the first drops of icy rain splattered down.

He opened his trailer door and stopped under the awning, thinking maybe he could make this quick and painless. One thing he was determined not to do was invite her in.

"You and I need to talk." Her gaze bored into him, harder than the drops of rain pelting down on the awning overhead.

"Later, I have to—"

"Now, unless you want to talk about your personal problems out here where everyone can hear," she said, then lowered her voice. "Problems like Keyes Hasting?"

He met her gaze, his blood turning to slush. "Why don't we step inside?"

THE WIND WHIPPED Faith's hair into her face as the storm moved in. The crowd scattered, everyone rushing to their cars or trailers as the rain fell hard as hailstones.

"Are you staying here again tonight?" her older sister asked as they ducked under Faith's trailer awning.

"We'll be shooting early in the morning if the weather clears up."

Eve hugged her again, running a hand over her blond hair just as she had done when they were children. "Be careful."

She started to say she was always careful. But look what had happened this morning. "I will."

"I'll be back tomorrow morning," Eve promised.

"That isn't necessary."

"Yes, it is." With that, her sister turned and hurried through the rain to her pickup.

Faith wondered where Jud was and swatted that thought away like a pesky fly. She wanted to talk to him about the accident earlier and the nagging feeling she had that it hadn't been the first on the set.

"Faith?"

She turned to see Nancy Davis coming toward her with the next day's call sheets.

"There are a few changes that affect you," Nancy said.

Faith took the sheet. "Nancy, I heard you were the one

who found Brooke after she was bitten by the rattlesnake. They say she would have died, if you and Jud hadn't acted quickly to get her to the hospital."

"Everyone should work more and talk less," Nancy snapped.

"I only mentioned it because it seemed so odd that she was bitten by a rattlesnake in her trailer. How in the world did the snake get in there?"

"I have no idea," Nancy said. "I have more important things to worry about." With that she turned on her heel and left.

Odd, Faith thought. No odder than Nancy herself, though.

"You okay?" asked a very male voice coming toward her. She turned to find Jud Corbett grinning at her.

"I heard you muttering to yourself. Is there a problem with the call sheet?"

She shook her head. "How well do you know Nancy Davis?"

"I *don't* know her. Why? Did one of your movie magazines say I dated her?" His grin broadened.

"You disappoint me. I thought you've dated everyone in Hollywood. Seriously, I'm curious about her." Faith told him what Nancy had just said.

Jud shrugged. "Appears she doesn't like being a hero. Why all these questions?"

"I saw your expression earlier when you asked me if I saw where the rock came from that spooked the wagon team. You think someone did it on purpose."

He held up his hands. "I never said that."

"Not in so many words. But you have to admit, Brooke getting bit by a rattlesnake in her trailer couldn't have been an accident. Snakes can't climb steps or open doors."

Jud hesitated. "Okay, that was suspicious. I think someone did it as a prank."

"A sick, dangerous prank."

"Few people die from snakebites. Brooke just happened to experience complications from the antidote."

"You're not fooling me for a minute, you know," she said. "You're scared someone is behind these accidents."

"Or maybe I wanted you to believe the accidents were deliberate so I'd have an excuse to protect you and spend every waking moment with you."

"Nice try."

"I'm serious, at least about wanting to protect you, and I can see now that spending time with you is the only way to keep you out of trouble. I have to go to the ranch tonight. Come with me." He held up his hands in surrender. "It's just dinner with my family. No ulterior motives." He grinned. "*Breakfast* isn't in the package."

She couldn't help but smile. The man was incredibly charming, and she hadn't been looking forward to being cooped up in her trailer.

"I have a stop to make in town first. I could meet you after that, say at Packy's?"

"Great," Jud said and grinned. "I hope you like Mexican food."

CHANTAL WAS ALL business as she stepped past the director into his trailer.

Zander glanced back through the pouring rain toward catering. A few people had taken cover under the huge canopy that sheltered the outdoor eating area. Some were looking in his direction. Even if they didn't hear what Chantal had said to him, he knew they were speculating on what was going. It wasn't like they didn't know about most of his *personal* problems.

He swore under his breath as he stepped into the trailer after his leading lady and slammed the door. Chantal had removed the lightweight jean jacket she'd been wearing. Rain droplets darkened the jacket where she'd hung it over the back of one of his chairs.

The woman herself was at his bar in the small kitchen making herself a drink.

"Scotch, straight up," he ordered. "Since you're pouring," he added when she turned, cocking a brow at his tone.

Zander slouched into the recliner, wondering what Chantal wanted and what she planned to offer in return. He'd been waiting for her to throw herself at him. Chantal Lee had warmed the couches of every director she'd worked with, her exploits as legendary as the remunerations she'd wriggled out of them.

Sex was the last thing on his mind as she handed him his drink and curled up on his couch. She ran a finger around the rim of her crystal tumbler and studied him openly.

"Why don't you cut to the chase," Zander said irritably. He'd never taken Chantal for a woman with brains as well as beauty, but as he met her gaze he wondered if he'd been wrong about that.

"I heard something that has me concerned," she said, still watching him with her laser-intense gaze.

Nothing he loved more than being forced to squash some stupid rumor on the set. "Whatever it is, it isn't true."

"Really?" One perfect brow arched upward. Chantal was like a giant cat curled up on his couch. She looked friendly enough, but he knew she could be purring one moment and scratching out his eyes the next.

"Then you didn't give me the leading role in this film because someone is blackmailing you?"

Zander choked on his Scotch.

"Faith." Sheriff Carter Jackson rose from behind his desk as his sister-in-law stepped into his office. Outside, lightning splintered the dark sky followed by booms of thunder that rattled the windows as rain fell in a torrent. "I heard about the excitement out on the set. You all right?"

She nodded, shook the rain from her and took the chair he offered across from him. She wasn't surprised he'd heard about the wagon incident. Probably from Eve.

"The accident is one of the reasons I'm here," Faith said. Now, though, she was having second thoughts. Spying on the people she was working with didn't seem like a good idea. Especially if there was even a chance her accident had been anything but.

Carter was waiting.

"I was wondering if you could do some checking for me? Unofficially?"

"What kind of checking?"

"I'm curious about the people I'm working with." She knew the scuttlebutt from movie magazines. What she needed was the behind-the-scenes kind of information that only a law enforcement person could provide.

Reaching in her pocket, she drew out the list of names she'd jotted down before coming in. Erik Zander, Chantal Lee, Nevada Wells, Brooke Keith, Jud Corbett.

She handed him the list.

His eyebrows shot up on the first name. "Erik Zander? He was involved in the death of a woman who drowned in a hot tub during a party at his Malibu residence."

"He was never arrested, right?" Faith asked.

"Not enough evidence," Carter said. "Not the same as being innocent, though."

Every tabloid in the country had picked up the story. What she found interesting was that the others on her list had been at that party, including Jud Corbett.

Carter scanned down the sheet and lifted his gaze back to her again. *"Jud Corbett?"*

Faith wished now she hadn't added his name to the list. "Those are the main people I work with. There is one more I forgot to add, Nancy Davis. From what I can gather, this is her first assistant director job."

"What is it exactly that you're looking for?" the sheriff asked, leaning back in his chair to study her.

"Accidents happen on movie sets all the time," she said quickly. "I think that's all this is. But it doesn't hurt to check out the primary people involved in the film, right?"

Carter sighed. "You sound like a cop. Okay. You'll let me know if there are any more accidents out there, right?"

"Of course," she said, feeling only a little guilty for coming here. She didn't want to betray Jud. Nor did she want anything to keep her from the stunt work on this film.

But she was no fool. Jud was holding something back. If there was a problem on the set, she wanted to know about the people she was working with.

Silently she prayed that the wagon incident would be the last. But a nagging feeling told her she wouldn't have come to the sheriff if she believed that.

Erik Zander wiped his mouth and said, "Blackmail? That's absurd." He downed the rest of his drink, his heart hammering wildly in his chest.

"So you weren't blackmailed into making this movie?"

"Hell, no. Where would you get such an outrageous idea?" he demanded.

She glanced down at the glass in her hand. He noticed she hadn't touched her drink while his was empty and he already needed another one.

He thought about asking her to get it for him, but his stomach was churning and he didn't trust himself to speak. Not that he expected she'd do it anyway.

When was he going to learn that there were no secrets in Hollywood? What a laughingstock he would be if this got out. The thought was so absurd, he snorted, making Chantal's head jerk up.

"What's so funny?" She looked irritated, as if he'd been making fun at her expense.

He shook his head. "Nothing." Here, just seconds ago, he'd been worried about being the laughingstock of Hollywood when Hasting had evidence that would make a jury send him to the electric chair. Did California have an electric chair, or would it be lethal injection? Hell, Hasting was probably going to kill him when this film was over and save the state the expense.

Was it any wonder Zander had totally lost his perspective?

"You know, if you really had been blackmailed into doing this picture, into giving me this role, then I have to wonder who else you were forced to hire." Chantal's gaze locked with his and he felt his stomach roil.

His head whirled. He held out his empty glass, hoping she'd take the hint.

She didn't. "That's the reason you gave Nevada the role, isn't it? Why else would you throw the two of us together in a film so soon after our breakup?"

Zander opened his mouth to tell her that he knew they

weren't really broken up, but nothing came out. He drew back his glass, which suddenly felt too heavy to hold.

"Which brings up the big question, doesn't it?" Chantal continued. "What could a blackmailer have on you that you'd let yourself be put in such a tenuous, not to mention dangerous, position?"

Zander leaned over to set his glass down on the coffee table. It slipped from his fingers and thudded onto the surface. Suddenly he didn't feel so good.

"Zander?" Chantal sounded far away.

He was having trouble catching his breath. His gaze shot to the table where he'd dropped his empty glass. It was gone. Chantal was standing over him, holding his empty glass and her own full one. No lipstick on the rim. She still hadn't taken a drink.

He opened his mouth, but only a rasping sound came out, each breath a struggle. He tried to get to his feet as he watched Chantal walk over to the sink, pour her drink down the drain and turn on the faucet to rinse her glass.

No! his mind screamed as she put her glass aside and rinsed out his, refilling it with water.

"Here, drink this," she said frowning as she came back over to him. Was that genuine concern in her voice? If so, then she was a better actor than he thought.

She'd poisoned him and he'd just sat here and watched her get rid of the evidence. Or had it been Hasting who'd put the poison in the Scotch this morning and Chantal had just stupidly destroyed the evidence, not realizing what she was doing?

He shoved the glass of water away and tried again to stand. He had to keep her from getting rid of the bottle of Scotch, the only proof left.

The room swam. He struggled to his feet, doubling over as he fought to catch his breath.

"Erik? You bastard, don't you dare have a heart attack and die before I get what I want."

He pitched forward, sprawling face-first on the floor. From far away he heard Chantal screaming. Down the hall, he caught sight of the doll he'd found on his bed last night. It was lying on the floor where he'd tossed it, those dark sightless eyes staring at him.

The doll appeared to be smiling.

Chapter Seven

"A panic attack?" Chantal stormed around her trailer, too angry to sit. "That's all Erik had? He scared me half to death. I thought he was having a heart attack."

"Apparently you scared him, as well," Nevada said from the couch. He'd come from the hospital emergency room where Zander had been rushed by helicopter earlier. "He thought you'd *poisoned* him."

She swung around. *"What?"*

Nevada nodded, smiling. "The moment Erik regained consciousness he had his girl Friday Nancy rush back out here to his trailer to retrieve the glass and bottle of Scotch that you used to pour his drink."

"And?"

"The Scotch bottle had mysteriously disappeared, along with both glasses the two of you had drunk from."

She stared at him. "I thought you said it was a panic attack?"

"It was. The hospital ran a blood test on him, and there was no poison in his bloodstream." Nevada shook his head.

"Then why would anyone get rid of the Scotch and glasses?"

He shrugged. "It's crazy since obviously the Scotch didn't affect *you*."

"I never got a chance to drink mine," she said.

"How *fortunate*," Nevada said.

"You think I put something in his Scotch?" she demanded incredulous. "That's why you declined a drink when I offered you one a minute ago."

"A man can't be too careful around a woman like you."

She grabbed a nearby couch pillow and threw it at him. He ducked and grinned. She reminded herself that she needed him to believe she gave a crap about him. "If you weren't so handsome…"

He ate that up. Usually. But not now. "Maybe there was something in the Scotch that normal blood test screening wouldn't find," he suggested, eyeing her. "Without evidence there is no way to prove his Scotch was doctored."

"You seem to know a lot about blood screening," she commented. "If his Scotch was 'doctored' then it happened before I got to his trailer. His door wasn't locked."

"Doesn't matter. The doctors say it was a panic attack and Zander overreacted. So you're off the hook."

"I was never *on* the hook." He was starting to irritate her.

"Erik might disagree with that, my love," Nevada said. "Unless you can produce the Scotch and glasses, I'm afraid you'll always appear guilty of something."

"You find that amusing?"

"No, I find that frightening," he said. "And exciting. I always knew you were a dangerous woman. Now I know just how dangerous."

"Someone took the bottle and glasses to incriminate me," she said.

"Or save you," he added. "Calm down. You're in the clear. Erik had a panic attack. And come on, he has reason to panic, the way this movie is going. I just saw Keyes Hasting talking to Nancy. What is he doing here?"

"Isn't it obvious? He's got money in this film," she said, not happy to hear that Nancy had been talking to Hasting. She hated not knowing what was going on.

"Erik wouldn't take money from Hasting," Nevada said. "Not unless—"

"He was desperate? Zander's career is riding on this film."

"And so is ours," he reminded her, as if she needed reminding. A few films that did poorly at the box office and the phones quit ringing. The only thing that had kept her name in the news was her breakup with Nevada.

He stood now and walked to the door as if leaving. She felt a moment's relief. Instead, he locked the door and turned back to her.

"What do you think you're doing?" she demanded as he strode to her, pulled her out of her chair and began to unbutton her blouse.

She tried to shove his hands away. "Everyone knows you're in here with me."

Nevada grabbed the front of her shirt and jerked. Buttons went flying, fabric tore. Roughly he cupped her right breast and squeezed as he gave her a punishing kiss.

She fought to push him away, both of them falling backward. The chair crashed to the floor, them right behind it.

"Stop it, you bastard!" she bellowed.

Above her, Nevada Wells smiled. "What did I ever see in a bitch like you?" he yelled as he bared her breasts.

Chantal grabbed the lamp cord and jerked it. The lamp crashed to the floor. She let out an obscenity as her hands went to the zipper of his jeans. Only a few more days and *Death at Lost Creek* would be over and she wouldn't need Nevada Wells anymore. But in the meantime…

MARY ELLEN HAD BARELY made it back to the motel in her rental SUV on the narrow muddy road. Now, as she looked out the window she saw that the rain still fell in a curtain of cold and poured from the rusted motel-room gutters like Niagara Falls. Through the darkness of the stormy afternoon she could see the huge droplets dimpling the ever-expanding puddles.

She'd planned to leave Whitehorse, to return to Billings, to catch any flight out of Montana that she could get on a moment's notice.

But those plans had changed as she drove back from the movie set. A thunderstorm like nothing she'd ever seen had swept in. *A gully washer.*

She blinked and could almost hear those words come out of her father's mouth. She let the curtain fall back over the window and turned to face the desolate motel room.

Rain or no rain, she couldn't stand to spend another moment in this room with nothing but her memories—and regrets. Everything about this town brought back the last time she'd been here.

Grabbing her suitcase and car keys, she pulled on her coat and, opening the motel room door, ran through the rain to the SUV. Once behind the wheel, she started the engine and turned on the heat to clear the windshield. Her coat was soaked and steaming up the windows faster than the heater could warm to clear them.

As if that wasn't bad enough, Mary Ellen noticed her gas gauge. She couldn't leave here without getting fuel—

not with a three-hour drive ahead of her and only two small towns between here and Billings.

She drove beneath the railroad underpass, coming up on Central Avenue, headed south of town on Hwy 191. Her wipers clacked loudly, unable to keep up with the driving rain.

At the last gas station on the edge of town, Packy's, she pulled into the pumps and sat in her car, waiting for the rain to let up a little before she got out to fill her tank.

As she was sitting there, a pickup pulled in on the other side of the pumps. To her shock, Eve Bailey Jackson got out and began filling the truck's gas tank. She wore a cowboy hat, jeans and boots and a slicker and seemed oblivious of the rain.

Mary Ellen wondered what Eve was thinking about as she finished getting gas and went inside to pay.

In the glow of warm light inside the small old-fashioned convenience store, Eve visited for a few minutes with the young woman behind the counter. Mary Ellen couldn't tell what Eve was saying. It didn't matter. She watched her, mesmerized.

"God help me," she whispered, tears welling in her eyes, as Eve Bailey Jackson came out.

Their gazes met for a moment through the rain. Eve slowed her step, frowned, and for a moment Mary Ellen feared she would come over to the car.

Hurriedly, Mary Ellen started her engine and pulled away as Eve walked to her truck and, still standing in the rain, watched as Mary Ellen drove away.

FAITH'S CELL PHONE RANG. She smiled as she saw who it was. "Hello?"

"How're your chores going?" Jud asked. "I was hoping we could meet in an hour."

The last thing she should be doing was having dinner

with Jud and his family. But she was curious about him. Curious about his family. "See you then."

She'd barely hung up when she got a call from her brother-in-law.

"I did that checking you asked for," the sheriff said.

"That was fast."

"Stop by my office if you want to see what I came up with. Nothing raises a red flag other than that trouble with the director. It apparently wasn't his first encounter with the law."

When Faith stopped by the sheriff's office, Carter wasn't in, but he'd left an envelope for her. She didn't open it until she reached her pickup.

Inside was a page of information on each of the people she'd asked him about. She scanned it, disappointed. Most of the information was the same as what she'd read in the movie magazines.

In the old days, movie stars often changed their names for Hollywood. That was less likely now. Nevada's parents had been involved in show business and had given each of their children "star" names.

Chantal Lee was actually Chantal Leigh Olsen. Brooke Keith had changed her name from Samantha Brooke Keifer. Nancy Davis was just Nancy Davis.

Nothing new about Jud. He was one of five brothers, raised on a ranch in Texas, started riding horses at the age of two.

Faith started to put the pages away when something caught her eye. Nancy Davis and Brooke Keith were both from the same small town in Idaho.

Looking up through the rain, Faith blinked. Nancy Davis had just pulled up in front of the *Milk River Examiner* and was now getting out of the SUV. The timing was too perfect.

As the assistant director ducked into the local newspaper office, Faith climbed out of her pickup and ran through the rain after her.

Like a lot of businesses in the small Western town, the newspaper didn't just offer news. It sold office supplies, offered photo processing and displayed the latest fund-raiser auction items in its front window.

Nancy turned as she heard the door open behind her and quickly checked her expression, but not before Faith had seen dread in the woman's face. Nancy wasn't happy to see her.

Since Faith had come on the film, Nancy had been cordial and businesslike. But definitely not friendly. Faith had wondered if it was because she'd taken Brooke's job. Or if Nancy was just that way, since she seemed to keep her distance from everyone on the set.

"Hi," Faith said to her and pretended interest in a loose-leaf notebook.

Andi Blake came out of the back of the newspaper office to wait on Nancy. Andi was dating Cade Jackson, the sheriff's older brother.

"Hi, Andi. I didn't know you were working here again," Faith said to the pretty Southerner.

"I'm a reporter again." Andi had been a big-city TV anchor before coming to Whitehorse as a reporter and falling in love with Cade.

Faith noticed the diamond engagement ring on Andi's finger. "Congratulations! When did that happen?"

"Just last night," Andi said, blushing. "We haven't had a chance to tell anyone yet."

"Don't worry, it's Whitehorse. By now, word is already circulating."

Andi laughed. "You're probably right. Several of the members of the Whitehorse Sewing Circle were in this morning, so I guess the announcements have been sent.

Heard about you working as a stuntwoman on the film and your accident this morning."

"Excuse me?" Nancy said impatiently. "Erik Zander asked me to pick up some old newspapers for the film set?"

"Sorry, I thought you two were together. Just give me a moment. I'll get them." Andi disappeared into the back again.

Faith didn't like Nancy being rude to Andi, who would soon be family, but she hid her feelings as she asked, "Do you have to get right back to the set? I was hoping we could have a cup of coffee."

Nancy looked surprised, then suspicious. "Erik is waiting for—"

"Just a quick cup. I wanted to ask your advice on something."

Nancy raised a brow, but said nothing as Andi returned with a large manila envelope.

"These are replicas of newspapers from the years he asked for," Andi said. "Should I put that on the movie account?"

"Yes, thank you." Nancy shoved the envelope into her large satchel as she turned to Faith. "I suppose I have time for a quick cup of coffee."

Faith told Andi goodbye and she and Nancy walked down the street to the small coffee shop. This time of the day the place was empty. They sat by the window. Nancy gave her a wry smile as she picked up the latte the waitress had put in front of her. "So it's advice you want?"

Faith had thought about breaking the ice by asking Nancy's advice about a career in movies, a ruse she realized the woman would have seen right through.

"I hope this isn't going to be more nonsense about Brooke's snakebite," Nancy said.

"No," Faith said. "But it is about Brooke."

Nancy frowned.

"She mentioned that the two of you went to school together in your hometown. Ashton, Idaho, right?"

All the color left Nancy's face. "Brooke told you that?"

"I'm pretty sure she's the one who mentioned it. Why? Is it a secret?" Faith chuckled as if she'd made a joke.

"Of course not. It's just not true."

"Really?"

Nancy seemed flustered. "Well, I mean, I guess she is from Ashton originally, too, but we didn't know each other."

"Oh, I just assumed you were friends, since it's a small town and you're both about the same age…."

"We went to the same school, but Brooke moved to California our junior year," Nancy said. "I never really knew her."

"So the two of you have never discussed being from the same town?"

"No, this is the first movie we've worked on together, and we have no reason to reminisce about Idaho. I'm sure she's as glad to be out of there as I am."

Nancy seemed to realize what she'd said. "Not that there is anything wrong with Idaho or Montana, it's just… I really have to go." She rose from the table, then hesitated.

"My treat," Faith said, even though Nancy had made no move to pay for their coffees.

"I know it wasn't advice you were after when you invited me for coffee, but I'm going to give you some anyway. Stop being so nosy. None of this has anything to do with you."

Without another word, Nancy turned and walked out. Faith stared after her. None of what had nothing to do with her?

She remembered what the sheriff had said about Zander having an earlier brush with the law and pulled out the papers he'd given her. Apparently there'd been another unfortunate accident that resulted in a death years ago. This one a car accident. Erik Zander had been driving.

A young woman had been killed. That time, too, he escaped being brought up on charges, although it was rumored that he'd been drinking and that the young woman was pregnant.

Sounded like history repeating itself if Erik Zander had been the father of that baby, as well.

That death had happened more than twenty years ago.

Faith paid for the coffee and went out to her pickup before she dialed the sheriff's office. When Carter came on the line she said, "Thanks for the information you left me."

"I warned you there wasn't much to find."

"I'm curious about something else, though. That incident involving the car wreck and Erik Zander twenty-some years ago, can you get me more information on it?"

"What are you doing?" Carter asked with a sigh.

"Satisfying my curiosity."

Carter said something under his breath she didn't catch. It had sounded like, "You damned Bailey girls."

"I'll see what I can find out. There won't be much since Zander was never charged."

Just like in the hot tub death twenty years later.

"Faith, I'm a little concerned about what you might be getting yourself into with this," her brother-in-law continued.

"Oh, come on, Carter, what could be more dangerous than being a stuntwoman?" she joked.

"You have a point there," he said. "Just be careful."

"Not to worry. I am always careful."

"Sure. Just like your sisters. And just as stubborn as them, too."

Driving down to Packy's to meet Jud Corbett she reminded herself that she and her sisters had that in common—curiosity. It had gotten them in trouble more times than she could remember. It had almost gotten both her sisters killed.

THE SCOTCH BOTTLE and the two glasses weren't the only things missing, Erik Zander had found out when he returned to his trailer.

That damned doll was gone. It had been the last thing he'd seen before he'd passed out, and now it was nowhere to be found.

He glanced out his window and saw Nancy returning. He tried to remember what he'd sent her to town to get for him. Whatever it had been, she didn't seem all that anxious to bring it to him.

"Erik?" Nancy looked surprised to see him standing at her trailer door. "I was going to bring you the old newspapers you had me get." She picked up a manila envelope and held it out to him.

He didn't take it.

"Erik? Is something wrong?"

He glanced over his shoulder and saw some of the crew standing a few yards away. "Can I come in?"

"Of course." She moved aside to let him enter. He closed the door behind him, then stood for a moment wishing he hadn't been so impulsive. *Just take the damned envelope and leave well enough alone.*

If he asked her about the doll, she was bound to wonder why he was making such a big deal out of a damned rag doll. It would be all over the set that he believed the evil of Lost Creek was real. Everyone was probably already talking about him after his so-called panic attack.

"Is there something else?" Nancy asked. She looked

flushed, even upset. Since she never got rattled, he wondered if something had happened in town.

Not that he cared what had her stirred up. He had too many problems of his own. His throat felt dry. He would have killed for a drink—if he hadn't been afraid to take one.

"I wanted to ask you if you took anything from my trailer," he blurted out.

Her eyes narrowed. "You asked me to take the Scotch bottle and the two used glasses, but like I told you, they weren't there when I looked for them."

"Not that." He glanced around her trailer, surprised how neat it was. He realized he didn't know this woman, certainly hadn't recognized her name when he'd been blackmailed into making her assistant director on this film. Was she Hasting's spy on the set? She seemed a bit…weak for the part.

"I thought I saw something on the floor of the bedroom right before I passed out," he said regretting this. "You didn't find anything?"

"What did you think you saw?"

He waved a hand through the air. "It's not important."

"Erik," she said as he turned to leave. "I didn't find anything out of place when I searched your trailer for the Scotch and glasses you and Chantal used."

He nodded and pushed open the door. Whoever had gotten rid of the glasses and Scotch had also taken the doll. But why? Someone had entered the trailer after he was flown to the hospital.

Not Nancy, since she'd flown with him in the chopper to the hospital. That left Hasting, Nevada, Chantal and Brooke. All of them had been in his trailer just that morning before his soon-to-be-legendary panic attack.

"Who has keys to the trailers?" he asked as a thought struck him.

"The occupants."

"The company that rents them must keep an extra. They didn't give you a master key?"

She frowned. "No. No one has a key to your trailer but you and the rental company. Why? Have you lost your key? I didn't think you ever locked the door."

He didn't.

"I tried it this morning when I came over. It was open," she explained, looking embarrassed. "It was open when I came back. Anyone could have gone in. I'm sorry I didn't think to lock it."

He stared at her. She was so damned competent. He didn't know what he would have done without her. Hell, she was the one that got both him and Brooke to the hospital before they'd died. He stared at her, seeing her maybe for the first time.

Something about the way she was looking at him nudged a memory. Maybe he had worked with her before and just forgotten. Or maybe they'd met somewhere else....

"Erik? Are you sure you're all right?"

He shook his head as his skin went cold and clammy, the contents of his stomach recoiling. He suddenly felt sick. Stumbling down her trailer steps, he aimed himself at his own trailer, hoping he could reach it in time.

MARY ELLEN DROVE AROUND aimlessly until she realized she hadn't had anything to eat all day and was weak and sick with hunger.

The only place open at this hour was a convenience store on the west end of town. She went in and got herself a cup of coffee and a sweet roll. It was too late to head for Billings, even if she could leave.

She knew she should go back to the motel and get some

sleep, but she couldn't rid herself of the image of Eve's face peering at her through the pouring rain. That startled look haunted her.

What had *Eve* seen? A resemblance to her own face? How long had Eve looked for that in every older woman's face, hoping to see her mother looking back?

Mary Ellen paid for the sweet roll and coffee and went back to her car. She forced herself to choke down the roll, knowing she needed sustenance, but unable to taste a bite. Washing down the last of it, she told herself she had to end this.

For years she'd lived with the lies and deceit. She couldn't do it any longer. But telling the truth would mean not only confessing to what she'd done, but also reliving her sins. She'd never been able to face those horrible memories, and yet she'd never been able to escape them, either.

Mary Ellen stared out through the rain, chilled at the sound of it drumming on the car roof. It was too late to do anything tonight. But if she waited she might lose what little courage she had.

She pulled out her cell phone and called Eve Bailey Jackson's number.

The phone rang once. Mary Ellen's hand shook and she almost snapped the cell shut as the phone at the other end rang a second time.

"Hello?" A woman's voice. Eve's?

Mary Ellen swallowed, her throat almost too dry to make a sound. "Eve Bailey Jackson?"

"Yes?"

"My name is Mary Ellen." She swallowed. "Mary Ellen *Small.* Your mother was my sister."

Chapter Eight

Jud had thought about calling ahead to let his family know he was bringing Faith to dinner.

But he didn't want anyone making a big deal of out it. If he made it sound like a spur-of-the-moment invitation, maybe his family wouldn't try to read anything more into it.

He'd told Faith the truth: he didn't like leaving her alone on the set. What he hadn't told her was that he thought he'd seen something right before the team of horses had been spooked. Movement on the fringe and something flying through the air. A rock? He couldn't be sure. And that's what worried him.

But his gut instinct told him that someone had intentionally caused the horses to spook. Had they known, though, that the team would take off and nearly kill Faith? Or had they thought it was Chantal sitting on the wagon, since that's who was supposed to be there at that moment according to the call sheet?

He didn't want to believe the accident had anything to do with Faith. Whoever was deliberately causing the accidents on the set had to be trying to sabotage the film. Why anyone involved in the movie would want to sabotage it was anyone's guess.

Or maybe it had been just a few unlucky accidents and he was making too much of it because he'd gotten Faith into this and now felt he had to keep her safe.

As he and Faith drove through the rain toward Trails West Ranch, Jud was glad to lose himself in the landscape. It was July, the wet grass was still a vibrant green that ran from horizon to horizon.

It surprised him how the land up here had gotten into his blood. When he'd thought of Montana, he'd always thought of snowcapped mountain peaks and towering pine trees—not the prairie with the only mountains in the distance and few if any pines.

But he liked that thousands of buffalo used to race across this expanse of earth and that outlaws holed up in the Missouri Breaks badlands. One of Butch Cassidy's and the Sundance Kid's alleged last robberies took place just outside of Whitehorse. Sometimes he thought he could feel the history as if it was entrenched in the landscape.

He noticed that Faith seemed content to stare out at the country, as well. Probably had a lot on her mind. He didn't mind not talking. He liked the sound of the rain on the roof of the pickup, the steady slap of the wipers, the sound the tires made as they churned up rainwater from the puddles.

"Where will you go after this?" Faith asked after a while. She'd been gazing out the window, looking at the land with a longing he recognized only too well.

"Wherever the next film takes me." Her gaze had shifted to him. He didn't tell her that he had a few months to kill. The downtime was the hardest. He tended to get into trouble, and that trouble usually involved a woman because, ultimately, he always left them to pursue his stunt work.

"What about you?" he asked, glancing over at her.

She shrugged, a secret smile turning up her lips. "I never thought I'd be doing what I am now, so who knows?"

She wore jeans, boots and a Western blouse that made him too aware of her curves. Her blond hair was pulled up into a ponytail and there was just the faintest touch of makeup, a brush of mascara to her lashes, a little gloss to her lips. The high color of her cheeks was all her own, he thought with a smile.

While Faith had earlier resembled Chantal enough to play her body double, right now she looked nothing like the leading lady.

There was an innocence about Faith that Chantal couldn't even act—and a peace, a self-assurance that he'd seen that first day when he'd caught her doing horse tricks on the back forty.

Now he realized too late that this was exactly the kind of woman his father would like to see him marry. Taking her home could be a huge mistake.

"There's something I need to tell you," he said, and cleared his throat. "I…the thing is, about my family…"

"I'm sure they're no worse than mine," she said, humor in her voice.

"Yeah." He smiled at that. "I just need to fill you in before we get there."

"Will I need a scorecard to keep track?" she asked, turning in the seat to face him.

He gave her a quick rundown of the family, from Juanita, the family cook who his father had convinced to come to Montana with them, to his four brothers, Russell, Dalton, Lantry and Shane.

"Shane's engaged to Maddie Cavanaugh, right?" Faith said.

"Yeah. But I'm not sure Maddie will be there tonight," he said, wondering how much he should tell her. "I believe this will become common knowledge soon enough… Kate, my dad's wife, is Maddie's birth mother."

"She's adopted? I had no idea."

"Not even Maddie knew. So things have been a little tense between Maddie and Kate."

"And Shane?"

"They'll work it out. They're perfect for each other, and since I'm the one who got them together…"

"I can't see you playing Cupid," Faith said, grinning.

"Well, that's another thing I need to tell you."

She laughed. "I need to know all this before having dinner at the ranch with your family?"

He was glad she found humor in it. He wished he did.

"Yeah, actually, you do. You see there's a chance my family might get the wrong idea about you and me."

She cut her eyes to him.

He held up a hand. "Not because of me. It's because of these letters my mother left before she died." He explained about his mother's dying wish that her sons marry before the age of thirty-five and marry a Montana cowgirl.

"You drew straws?" She sounded as incredulous as he'd been at the suggestion at the time.

"You had to have been there. The letters, Dad's recent marriage, the move to Montana, this family code we have, it put a lot of pressure on us. I know Dad just wants us all to settle here so we can be closer as a family."

"Realistically, do you see that happening?"

"Hell, no. Nor do I have any plans to get married anytime soon."

"But you drew the shortest straw and there's that family code of yours." She smiled, clearly having fun with him.

"Laugh if you will, but I just wanted to warn you so you know what you might be walking into."

"You're afraid they'll think I'm your date—or worse, your *girlfriend*."

"I'm glad you're enjoying yourself at my expense."

"I had no idea dinner with you and your family could be this…interesting," she said, smiling at him as the ranch came into view.

Trails West Ranch was nestled in a valley of green, the badlands of the Missouri Breaks in the distance. At the center sat the ranch house.

Jud slowed, glanced over at Faith and wondered if it would be so bad if the family thought Faith was his date.

EVE BAILEY CLUTCHED the phone in her hand. "Mary Ellen *Small?* If this is some kind of joke…"

"You called my mother, Mary, looking for a woman named Constance Small. She called me after she hung up with you."

Eve was at a loss for words. "I don't understand." Her voice broke.

"My younger sister was your mother."

"How do I know that's true?" she asked, even as she remembered the woman she'd seen at Packy's earlier, that feeling of seeing someone she knew, a stranger with a face that had seemed so familiar…

"I brought all the proof you'll need with me, but are you sure you want to know? You may not like what I have to tell you."

Eve felt as if her heart might burst. After all this time, could it be true? "Yes, I've waited for thirty-four years. I'm *sure*."

"It's late. Perhaps we could meet in the morning."

"No, I need to see you now. This can't wait any longer, *please*."

"All right. I doubt either of us will get any sleep tonight anyway. Do you want me to come there?"

"I'll come to you."

"I'm staying at the Riverview Motel. Number six."

"I'll be there in ten minutes." Eve hung up, her heart pounding. Was it possible she was finally going to find out the truth?

But if so, then why hadn't Constance Small come herself? Why send her sister? *Your mother* was *my sister.* That's what the woman had said. Did that mean her mother was dead?

There was only one way to find out. She had so many questions. Eve grabbed the keys to her pickup and headed for the door. Ten minutes. In ten minutes she knew she would be facing the woman she'd seen at Packy's earlier.

Her aunt Mary Ellen Small? Finally someone from her birth family. Someone who resembled her.

Eve knew better than to get her hopes up. She'd been disappointed too many times before. As she drove the five miles into town to the Riverview, she wondered if she should let Carter know where she'd gone.

No. He'd be suspicious and want to come along, and this was something she had to do alone. She didn't even want her brother there, didn't want to get his hopes up until she knew for sure. In truth, she just needed this desperately for herself and had for as long as she could remember.

The rental SUV she'd seen earlier at Packy's was parked in front of room six, just as she knew it would be. Eve braced herself as she pulled in beside it and, cutting the engine, she got out and ran through the rain.

She was trembling with excitement and anxiety and cold dread. For so long she'd feared she would never know what happened the night she was born. Nor would she ever see another person who looked like her, who shared her blood, her coloring, her DNA.

Then her twin brother, Bridger, had come into her life. And she'd told herself it was enough. But she couldn't smother that need in her to find her birth mother. To know why the woman had given them up.

Eve feared Mary Ellen Small was right, that she wasn't going to like the answer, as she tapped at the motel room door, terrified.

The woman had asked her if she was sure she wanted to know the truth. Without hesitation, she'd said yes.

But now that Eve was this close to it, could she take the truth? What could hurt more than knowing your mother gave you up?

Nothing, she told herself as the door opened and she came face-to-face with a woman who looked so much like her that Eve began to cry.

FAITH FELT AT HOME right away. The Trails West Ranch house was warm and beautiful inside, the decor keeping with the area and the history of the ranch itself. The walls and floors were rich wood, the fireplace stone and the furnishings Western.

Grayson Corbett was as charming as his son and equally as handsome. He greeted her warmly and then introduced her to his wife, Kate.

She was a striking woman and Faith immediately saw the resemblance between her and Maddie Cavanaugh.

"You brought a date?" asked a male voice as Faith was led into a large family room that looked out over the ranch. It was furnished with soft, deep leather chairs and a bar stocked better than any saloon in town.

"My brother Dalton," Jud said with a sigh. "Meet Faith Bailey. She's a local who's doing stunt work on the film."

Faith shook hands with Dalton and saw three other brothers rise to their feet for introductions, all of them equally gorgeous.

"I heard the other stuntwoman was bitten by a rattlesnake," Kate said. "Is she all right?"

"She's fine. She'll be helping with the stunts," Jud was saying behind her.

"Lantry Corbett. I'm the smart, good brother," he said, shaking Faith's hand. "And this is Shane and Russell."

Faith recognized Shane. Now that she thought about it, she recalled seeing Shane dancing with Maddie Cavanaugh at a rodeo last month at the fairgrounds.

Russell seemed the most reserved of the brothers, as Grayson asked what she'd like to drink and Faith found herself in the middle of all the Corbetts sipping an ice-cold margarita rimmed with salt and laughing at the antics of the "boys," as Grayson called his five sons.

Later, as she was led into dinner, the dining room smelled of corn tortillas and a wonderfully spicy sauce. By then, she'd warmed to all the Corbetts. Her only misgiving was that they did indeed believe she was Jud's date. She felt as if she were auditioning for a role in a Corbett film.

The worst part was that she knew by the end of the evening that she had the role if she wanted it. And that gave her more pleasure than it should have. But it also made her a little sad since she wasn't up for the part.

"I had fun tonight," she said on the drive back toward the movie location. "I like your family."

"They certainly liked you," Jud said, not sounding all that happy about it.

"I'm sorry if that causes you trouble."

He laughed softly. "Maybe I should try to line you up with one of my brothers. Just kidding," he said almost too quickly.

"Want to keep me all for yourself, huh? I don't know if I like that. That one brother of yours…"

"Don't even think about—" He broke off abruptly as he realized somewhat belatedly that she was only joking. "Not that one of them wouldn't *love* you," he said with a shake of his head. "But I'm through playing matchmaker."

They fell into a comfortable silence, the narrow two-lane road seeming endless. Faith felt close to Jud, the cab of his pickup pleasurably intimate. She still couldn't believe the twist of fate that had brought her to this moment in time.

"The stunt early tomorrow is an easy one," Jud said, as if wanting to get back on more secure footing. It had felt like a date tonight and she was sure that made him uncomfortable.

"I'm not worried," she said of the upcoming stunt and looked out at the night. The stunt was part of the love scene sequence. The heroine tries to outrun the hero on a horse. He catches her, drags her off her horse and into his arms for a passionate kiss. Faith's part would end once her feet touched the ground—just before the kiss.

As Jud pulled into Packy's beside her pickup, he said, "I'll follow you. Just in case you have any problems."

"I don't need you to protect me." Although she was touched.

"Too bad. Until this film is over, I'm stuck to you like glue."

Until the film was over, which wasn't long.

True to his word, he followed her out to the set. As she topped a rise, the lights of Jud's pickup right behind her, she spotted the film's base camp through the now drizzling rain below her and felt disappointed. In a few short minutes, this night would end.

When Jud turned off the charm, he was quite…well, charming, and seeing him with his family, he'd gotten to her tonight.

She drove down the hill and parked. He pulled in beside her and climbed out. They hurried to duck under the awning of her trailer, which was closest to where they'd both parked. She breathed in the damp scent of the rainy summer night as if she could hold on to it and this moment forever.

The night was cool enough that she would have been grateful to be in his arms. But Jud stood away from her, looking out at the dark circle of trailers, the light rain pattering on the awning over their heads.

"If for any reason you need my help, day or night—"

"Don't worry about me," she said, hugging herself. "I'll be fine."

"Just do me one favor," he said, turning toward her, keeping his voice low. "Please don't ask any more questions about the accidents."

The rainy darkness settled around them. Faith hadn't realized how late it was. Not a light glowed in the encampment, not a sound could be heard from any of the other trailers.

"Faith, please. Promise me."

Not wanting to spoil the evening, she said, "Trust me, I'll be good." She didn't say what she'd be good at. Nor did she completely understand why, like her sisters, she'd never been able to turn the other way when there was trouble. Or better yet, run.

"Thank you for a very enjoyable dinner," she said, but didn't move. Nor did Jud.

They stood staring at each other. For one incredibly

prolonged moment Faith thought he might kiss her good-night. Her heart was pounding so hard she feared it alone would rouse the whole place.

Jud took a step back, looking nervous, actually awkward, a strange sight considering the grace of the man.

Faith hurriedly opened her trailer door, realizing he was merely waiting until she was safely inside.

Once inside, she peeked out to see Jud walking off through the rain, shaking his head and muttering under his breath. She smiled to herself, touched by his concern for her and pretty sure a kiss had been on his mind, as well.

She hoped he was mentally kicking himself all the way back to his trailer.

EVE STARED through her tears at the woman standing in the motel-room doorway.

Mary Ellen Small stared back, tears welling in her dark eyes as she said, "You look even more like Constance up close. Please, come in." She stepped back to let Eve enter, her tone businesslike, but Eve saw a tremor in the woman's hands as she closed the door.

The room was like any other motel room, except this one was almost too clean and tidy, making Eve question how long the woman had been staying here.

"How long—"

"I got to town yesterday," Mary Ellen said. "I told myself I only came here to see you from a distance. I had no intention of actually meeting you, let alone talking to you about Constance."

Eve frowned. "What changed your mind?"

"I'm not sure. Won't you have a seat?" She indicated one of the chairs at a small table.

"I think I'm too nervous to sit," Eve admitted.

The woman smiled at that. "I made coffee. I thought we both might need a cup. Please sit down. We have time, don't we?"

"After waiting thirty-four years, what's a few more minutes?" She pulled out a chair and sat down as Mary Ellen Small poured two cups of coffee and using the lid of the plastic ice bucket carried them over to the table. She returned to bring back sugar and creamery packets, napkins and spoons, before she took the other chair.

"You said I look like my mother?" Eve said cradling the cup of hot coffee in both her hands for the warmth. She was shaking and needed something to anchor her.

Mary Ellen nodded, studying her. "It's quite shocking how much you resemble her. I see nothing of your father—" She broke off and looked away before concentrating on her coffee.

"You knew my father, then."

The woman took a sip of her coffee, then carefully put down the cup. "How much do you really want to know?" she asked, her gaze locking with Eve's for a long moment.

"Everything." It might be her only chance. Eve wasn't about to pass it up, no matter the outcome. "Not knowing is worse than anything."

"Maybe."

Suddenly Eve wanted Bridger here. "My twin brother. He'll want to hear this." She drew out her cell phone.

Mary Ellen covered her hand. "Why don't you decide if you want to tell him after you hear what I'm going to say."

Something in her tone made Eve hesitate. Bridger was so happy right now with his wife and infant son. He'd found peace. Until she knew what this woman had to tell her…

"All right," Eve said and tried to settle back into her chair, afraid Mary Ellen Small might be right. This might be something Bridger wouldn't want to hear. "Please, tell me about my mother and why she isn't the one telling me this."

As Faith turned away from the window and the image of Jud disappearing into the darkness near his trailer, she saw the doll.

It sat on the small kitchen counter, its black-stitched eyes staring blankly at the door—and her.

Faith started at the sight of it, stumbling back, her hand going to her mouth to hold back a scream. Only then did she realize her trailer door hadn't been locked moments ago.

But she'd made sure it was locked when she'd left to go into town. Someone must have the key. Someone who wanted to scare her by leaving one of those horrible rag dolls for her to find.

Her initial shock morphed into anger in an instant. Whoever had done this was wasting her time if she thought she could intimidate her. Nancy Davis. That's who it had to be. She must have spare keys for all the trailers since she seemed to be the director's go-to girl.

Faith was so furious she thought about confronting Nancy tonight, just storming over there with the doll in hand and beating on the assistant director's door.

She took a breath. Probably not the best approach, given that she still had to work with Nancy. No, the best thing to do would be to ignore it. Faith certainly wasn't buying into the dolls being harbingers of disaster.

Stepping to the kitchen counter, she picked up the doll and was surprised by her reaction to the touch. She *was* buying into all this heebie-jeebie stuff. Angry with herself as much as the person who'd left it, she tossed the doll into the trash.

For a few moments, she stood in the kitchen breathing hard, angry and scared. Cursing, she stepped to the door, locked it, then dragged a chair over and levered it under the handle. It wouldn't keep anyone with a key out, but if someone tried to come in, the chair would at least fall and warn her.

She tried to calm down, but her blood still ran hot and her skin clammy and chilled with apprehension.

Knowing she would pay hell getting to sleep after this, Faith decided to take a hot shower. She'd brought along a long white flannel nightgown, a birthday present from her mother that she'd never worn. Usually she slept in a soft, worn T-shirt and nothing else.

Tonight seemed like the perfect night for the old-lady nightgown and the new mystery novel she'd picked up in town. She'd be ready if she had another visitor.

FAITH WOKE with a start. She couldn't remember falling asleep, but the mystery novel lay open beside her on the bed. She listened. The rain had stopped. Is that what had awakened her?

Whatever it had been, she knew she wouldn't be able to go back to sleep until she checked the trailer. She hated that the doll had spooked her. It was just a stupid, ugly doll. But it meant that someone on this set was trying to scare her.

Normally, she didn't scare easily, she thought, as she padded through the small trailer. The chair she'd put against the door was right where she'd left it. No one had broken in.

She glanced at her watch. A little after 1:00 a.m. For a moment, she stood in the middle of the living room. The curtains were all closed and she hadn't turned on a light. She moved through the dim darkness to the window that looked out on the other trailers and carefully drew back the curtain.

Low clouds hung over the camp, the moon illuminating them and casting the night in a silver glow. No lights shone in any of the trailers. She stared out into the night and yawned. Nothing moved in the eerie light.

As she started to let the curtain fall back into place, something caught her eye. A dark figure was standing behind one of the equipment trailers.

Faith's breath caught in her throat as she noticed there was what looked like a large bundle at the person's feet. She watched frozen in place as the figure bent down and began to pull on the large object.

A chill streaked up her spine as the two forms melted into the shadows behind the trailer.

The person appeared to be dragging a body.

Chapter Nine

Faith couldn't move, could barely breathe. She wanted to scream, to wake up the entire camp. But reminded herself that she couldn't trust her eyes. The stupid doll had left her jumping at shadows.

But if that wasn't someone dragging a body away from the camp, then what *had* she seen?

She stared out the window. The figure had dropped over a rise. If she just kept standing here… Faith moved quickly to the door, removing the chair, and opening her door to look out.

Seldom in her life had she been unable to make a decision. Better to make a wrong one than do nothing, had always been her motto. She looked down at what she was wearing. No time to change. She looked around for her boots and, giving up, stepped out of the trailer and started across the encampment in her bare feet.

Her instincts told her to go wake up Jud. But she feared that in the amount of time it would take to get him, the person would be gone. Not to mention how she would feel if it turned out she'd only imagined a person pulling a body away from camp.

There was that and the fact that Faith didn't trust herself

tonight. Or was it her imagination she mistrusted? Of course it couldn't have been a body. It must have been a bag of equipment.

But why would anyone drag a bag of equipment out toward the prairie in the middle of the night? Maybe someone robbing the set.

Faith needed to be sure she wasn't on a wild-goose chase. If she could just get a good look…

She sprinted barefoot across the open area to the edge of the trailer where she'd last seen the person and worked her way to the back. Squinting through darkness, she saw nothing. No movement. No person. No body.

She was on a fool's errand, she told herself as she slipped around the edge of the trailer into the blackness of the night. The clouds were so low she found herself walking through a foggy mist. This was crazy. Her feet were cold and wet, as was the hem of her nightgown. What was she doing?

Movement. She blinked, took a step and felt something squish between her toes. Mud. That's when she saw the tracks. Drag marks in the mud.

She shuddered. Turn back. Go get help. In the distance, she heard a noise. The distinct clank of a tailgate being dropped. To load whatever the person had been dragging. That meant the person had a vehicle parked out there.

Avoiding walking in the tracks, telling herself they could be evidence, she followed the drag marks through the mist.

As she topped a rise, she saw a light blink on ahead. A dome light in a vehicle parked down in a gully. Faith looked back and saw nothing but mist. She could make out only the tops of the trailers in the distance. If she yelled for help, she doubted anyone would hear her. All it would do is alert the person below her.

Crouching down, she edged her way into the gully. It was an old, dry creek bed, which made her sorry she hadn't at least taken the time to find her boots.

The pickup had been backed into a small bluff. No doubt to make dragging a body into the truck's bed easier. Faith couldn't see anyone around the pickup. The tailgate was still down but from where she was, she couldn't tell if anything had been loaded in the back.

So where had the person gone?

Holding her breath, she moved up the dry creek bed, each step painful barefoot.

The vehicle was one of the trucks rented for the movie crew. The driver's-side door was open, the dome light a dim glow inside the cab. No sign of anyone.

If it hadn't been for the tracks and the pickup, she might have been able to convince herself she'd imagined the whole thing.

But her instincts told her that there was a body in the back of that pickup. Maybe the person who'd dragged it out here had circled back to the camp for something. She had to move fast. Just get a look in the bed of the truck and hightail it back to the camp for help.

Faith edged closer, stepped on a sharp rock and almost cried out. She was within feet of the pickup. Just a little closer. The hair on the back of her neck stood up as she touched the wet, cold metal and leaned over the side to look into the bed of the truck.

The scream rose in her throat, but it didn't get a chance to escape as something hard and solid struck her temple. The night went black and empty.

THE MOTEL ROOM was deathly quiet in the late hour. Eve listened to the hum of the coffeemaker and her own pounding heart. If the woman sitting across from her hadn't looked so much like her, Eve would fear this was all a dream.

Or worse, a hoax.

"You must let me tell you in my own way," Mary Ellen said in her reserved tone. "This is very difficult for me." Her voice broke.

"I'm sorry," Eve said and tried to be patient.

A moment later, Mary Ellen put down her coffee cup and began. "Constance was the sweetest little baby. I was there the night she was born. She was one of those babies that hardly ever cried, smiled all the time. We all loved her and spoiled her. Maybe too much."

Eve waited, saying nothing as Mary Ellen seemed to need time to gain control again.

"Constance began to rebel in high school. I was two years older. I had always been such an obedient child, a straight-A student, the child who never caused any problems. Because of that my parents were at a loss as to what to do about Constance. She became more willful. Looking back, I'm sure she was rebelling because of me. She had always been in my shadow and because of that too much was expected of her. Her grades were never as good nor could she seem to stay out of trouble."

Mary Ellen seemed to brace herself. "I fell in love my senior year. I'd never even dated before that. Paul was—" Her voice broke. "Paul was everything I'd ever dreamed of. Handsome and sweet. We planned to marry after college. My parents adored him. Constance *idolized* him."

Eve felt dread growing inside her.

"Paul gave me an engagement ring on my eighteenth birthday." Mary Ellen smiled in memory. "The diamond was small, but I thought it was the most beautiful thing I'd ever seen."

Eve watched her take a sip of her coffee, aware there were no rings on the woman's slim fingers. Nor apparently had she ever changed her last name.

"For my high school graduation a few months later, my parents threw a party for me at our home. Paul had seemed upset that day. It wasn't until my sister came to me in tears…" Mary Ellen swallowed, her throat constricting for a moment. "She told me she was pregnant. That Paul was the father of her baby."

It felt as if all the air had been sucked out of the room. "You must have been horribly hurt," Eve said, feeling the weight of this woman's pain.

Mary Ellen lifted her gaze to Eve. "I was devastated." She took a breath and let it out. "I vowed to destroy Paul and my sister and the baby she carried."

JUD CORBETT COULDN'T fall asleep. He lay in the dark, thinking about Faith. About dinner. About almost kissing her. It was no wonder he couldn't sleep, given the emotions churning inside him.

What was it about the damned woman? He'd dated his share of beauties, women with talent and intelligence. But he'd never met one like Faith. She was beautiful, talented, intelligent, probably too intelligent, funny, compassionate, passionate and incredibly courageous to the point of concern.

He got up, wearing only his jeans, and padded to the front window to look out at her trailer. It wasn't the first time he'd done this tonight. But he promised himself it was the last. Maybe she couldn't sleep, either. If her light just happened to be on…

It wasn't. He started to let the curtain drop back into place when he saw her. Or at least her ghost.

He hurried to the door and out into the cold night. As

he ran to her he saw that her feet were as bare as his own. She wore a long, white nightgown, the hem and back muddy and wet like her feet.

"Faith?"

"Jud?"

"Faith, what are you doing out here in the rain?"

"I…" She looked around, rain running down her face. She shivered. "I was going… I don't know…"

"Were you sleepwalking?"

"I…guess so."

"Faith, you're bleeding."

He swung her up into his arms and carried her toward his trailer. She leaned into him. He listened to her steady breathing, reassured. What if he hadn't gotten up when he did and happened to see her?

Opening his door, he carried her inside to the bathroom. The shower stall was small and he knew from experience that there wouldn't be a lot of hot water in the tank. Setting her down, he saw that her eyes were shut.

"We have to get your wet nightgown off and get you into a hot shower, okay?"

She nodded, still looking confused.

Hurriedly, he turned on the shower and pulled her wet nightgown over her head. Pulling her to her feet, he stepped into the hot water with her still wearing his jeans.

It took the entire tank of hot water to warm her up. When the shower began to run cold, he carried her out to his bed and wrapped her in warm, dry towels, rubbing her skin gently and then covering her with the comforter.

"Feeling better?"

She nodded. "I just don't understand what I was doing out there."

"You must have been sleepwalking." He'd checked to

make sure the cut and bump on her head weren't serious enough to have a concussion.

"Don't worry about it. Just rest." She looked exhausted.

She nodded and closed her eyes.

He watched her sleep for a few minutes before he padded back to the bathroom and stripped out of his wet jeans.

Returning to the bedroom, he pulled on a pair of pajama bottoms from a pair he'd gotten for Christmas from one of his brothers. They had scantily clad girl trick riders on them. Appropriate, he thought as he looked down at Faith.

He lay down beside her, pulling her close to keep her warm. She snuggled against him, sighing in her sleep. He listened to her steady breathing, her body warm against his, and fell into a deep sleep.

EVE GASPED, unable to believe what Mary Ellen had just said about wanting to destroy her fiancé and her sister. "You were upset. The two people closest to you had betrayed you. But surely you wouldn't have…" The rest of the words caught in her throat at the look in Mary Ellen Small's dark eyes.

"I wanted to *kill* them," she said in a voice that chilled Eve to her soul. "Constance was crying, pleading with me to forgive her. I knew what she'd done. She'd wanted Paul only because he was mine, just as she coveted everything I'd ever had from my grades to my clothes to my car, all things I'd worked for while she only whined."

The bitterness Eve heard in the woman's voice made her pull away. She picked up her coffee cup, her hands trembling so hard that the now lukewarm coffee splashed onto her jeans.

Mary Ellen handed her a napkin. "You said you wanted to hear this. I can only tell you the truth."

Eve nodded, unable to find her voice, and Mary Ellen continued in that same eerie tone.

"I told Constance I would forgive her if she and Paul did something for me. They owed me. They were to meet me in the trees on the hill behind the house later that night. We agreed on a time and I went back down to my party."

Eve wondered at how the woman could have faced everyone after learning of such a betrayal, but said nothing.

"That night I took all the money I had and packed a suitcase for my sister. Downstairs, I got my father's gun from the cabinet where he hid it, loaded the gun and went into the woods. They were both there waiting for me."

Eve tensed, waiting.

"Paul was as remorseful as my sister. He begged my forgiveness. I told them there was only one way. They both had to leave town, never come back, never contact me or anyone we knew, never tell anyone about the baby. If they broke their part of the agreement, I would kill them. When I pulled out my father's gun, cocked it and pointed the barrel at Constance's head, they believed me." Mary Ellen said the words with such a lack of emotion that Eve shuddered.

"Are you telling me that you never heard from your sister again?" Eve had to ask when Mary Ellen didn't go on.

"I only wish that were true." She took a sip of her coffee her expression as bitter as the brew. "Constance broke the agreement six months later when she called my mother."

Eve waited.

Mary Ellen shook her head, her gaze distant as if lost in the past. "She left me no choice but to do what I had said I would do. I came to Whitehorse. My mother thought I was coming here to save my sister and bring her home. She still believes that. But, of course, that was the last thing I planned to do."

"You didn't *kill* her," Eve said, shaken. Otherwise Eve and her brother wouldn't be here now.

"No, I got there too late."

Eve shook her head. "You were young and hurt, but I don't believe you would have harmed her."

Mary Ellen smiled at that. "I had already harmed her by sending her away at that young age with Paul, who was only a few years older, forcing them to live apart from family and friends with nothing but each other and their shared guilt over what they'd done."

"They weren't entirely innocent."

"No, but I wanted them to suffer the way I suffered. I hoped it would destroy whatever they'd felt for each other and that the pregnancy would make matters worse. I got what I wanted. Constance told my mother she'd been living a nightmare. I took great enjoyment in that."

"I don't know that I wouldn't have done the same thing," Eve said. Her thoughts went to her husband, Carter, and how he had betrayed her when she was a senior in high school. She'd sworn she'd never forgive him. It had taken years. "I have a hard time forgiving."

Mary Ellen glanced at her watch. "There is much more to tell and it's so late. I'm weary. If I promise to tell you the rest tomorrow, will you trust me to do so?"

Eve looked into the woman's eyes, eyes so like her own.

"I can tell you that I never break a promise," Mary Ellen said.

Eve believed her. She nodded and rose.

"Leave your cup. I'll straighten up in the morning."

"What time shall I come back?"

"Ten. It will be good if we both get some rest."

Eve heard the warning in the woman's tone. Eve would need her rest before hearing the conclusion of this story. "I'll be here at ten."

MILES AWAY at the film encampment, a figure stood in the dark having watched as Jud Corbett took the new stunt-woman into his trailer.

A small faint light was still burning at the front of the trailer, but there hadn't been a sound coming from inside for almost an hour.

What had Faith Bailey told him? She couldn't have been in any shape to tell him much.

I shouldn't have turned my back on her. I thought she was out cold. Who knew she'd wake up so quickly and head back toward the camp?

It was the last that caused concern. If she'd been able to run away, if she was conscious enough to head in the right direction—back toward the camp, then she might have been cognitive enough to tell Jud what she'd seen.

But wouldn't he have called the sheriff, and wouldn't the sheriff have been here by now?

There was only one thing to do. Wait. Let Faith Bailey spill her guts. But who would believe her if there was nothing to find? Actually, this could be an advantage.

No reason to panic. Everything was going according to plan. This turn of events might work out perfectly.

There was just one fly in the ointment. If Faith Bailey became too much of a problem. Obviously the doll hadn't scared her enough to butt out.

She might need a stronger warning. Or if she became too much of a problem…well, accidents happened all the time on movie sets. She should have learned that with the runaway team.

And if Faith didn't talk…well, no one needed to know about tonight.

But if she continued to hang out with Jud, then she would be jeopardizing Jud Corbett as well as herself. And that would be a shame.

Chapter Ten

Faith woke wrapped in a warm cocoon to the sound of voices outside her trailer. She snuggled deeper, refusing to open her eyes. The room felt cold and she wasn't ready to get up.

For a few moments she couldn't remember where she was. She thought she was at her family's ranch house and that the voices she heard were her sisters downstairs making breakfast. She sniffed the air, hoping against hope for the smell of frying bacon. Pancakes would be good, too. With lots of butter and homemade chokecherry syrup. "Mmmmmm."

Someone stirred next to her.

With a jolt, she shot up in the bed and instantly felt light-headed, even before she glanced behind her and saw Jud Corbett, where only seconds before he'd been spooned against her.

"What in the—" She was fighting the covers trying to get out of the bed when he grabbed her.

"Easy. I can explain."

She blinked at him, then at the trailer. This wasn't hers. That meant— "What am I doing in your trailer?"

"You were sleepwalking. At least, I think that's what you were doing."

"Sleepwalking?" He had to be kidding. She hadn't sleepwalked since she was a child.

"I found you wandering around the camp in a white nightgown. You were soaked to the skin, muddy and freezing cold."

"And?" she asked, not sure she wanted to hear this part.

"And I put you in the shower, warmed you up—"

"Exactly how did you 'warm me up'?"

"With hot water, then I dried you and put you into my bed and covered you up."

"That's it?"

"What? Did you expect me to take advantage of you?" She narrowed her eyes at him.

"I'm insulted," he said, drawing back from her. "You really don't trust me, do you? No, don't answer that. It's obvious," he said, getting out of bed.

She noted that he wore pajama bottoms—not that it necessarily proved anything. Glancing down, she saw that she was naked. She pulled the comforter up to her chin. "Where are my clothes?"

"I just told you. All you were wearing was a white night-gown. I hung it up to dry in the bathroom." He moved to the accordion door that separated the living room from the so-called master bedroom/bathroom. "Check if you don't believe me."

She waited until he closed the door all the way before she climbed out of bed and padded into the bathroom. Just the sight of her muddy white nightgown gave her pause. A memory flirted at the edge of her consciousness.

Shivering, she recalled being cold and muddy and…hurt. She stumbled to the mirror over the sink, her fingers going to the bandage on her temple. As she drew back her hand, she realized that Jud might actually be telling the truth.

She'd sworn that he'd never get her into his bed—and he had. But apparently nothing had happened. Unless you considered the fact that he'd stripped her naked and apparently given her a shower, dried her and put her to bed.

She was no prude, but if Jud was going to see her naked, this scenario wouldn't have been her first choice.

"You all right in there?" he called through the thin door.

"Yes." She felt embarrassed for being angry with him, since apparently he'd saved her. Again. Now she was embarrassed on general principle. "Thank you."

"No problem." He sounded gruff. She couldn't really blame him, since she'd questioned his integrity.

"I'm sorry."

"I'm sure it came as shock to wake up next to me."

Something like that.

She could hear people moving around in the camp. She pulled down her nightgown from where he'd hung it to dry. It was still damp. Along with the mud, there was some blood. Her blood, apparently.

"I can't go out like this," she said, glancing down at her naked body and feeling herself flush at the thought of Jud Corbett's hands touching her. Damn, she wished she hadn't missed that.

"I could go to your trailer and get you some clothing. If that's all right. I'll be as discreet as possible."

"That would be nice." She was going to be seen coming out of his trailer. There would be no getting around that.

As she waited for him to return, she found herself staring again at her nightgown. Bits and pieces of memory played tag in her brain. Just when she thought she could catch hold of one and make sense of it, the darned thing escaped.

She stopped trying so hard, convinced that, given time, it would all come back.

Jud returned and handed her two filled plastic bags through the door. Inside she found a black lace bra and matching panties. Had she been the kind of girl who blushed, she was sure she would have. He'd also brought her a pair of jeans, socks, boots and a Western shirt.

She drew on the clothing, stuffed the soiled nightgown into one plastic bag and opened the door between the rooms. The smell of coffee dragged her like a lasso into the kitchen.

Without a word, Jud handed her a cup. "No reason to go tearing out of here. Everyone's at breakfast." In other words, in plain sight of his trailer.

She nodded, said "thanks" and took the cup. The coffee tasted heavenly. "You're a lifesaver." She meant it because of the coffee, but she realized it covered the situation pretty well.

"How do you feel?" he asked, motioning for her to take the small recliner while he took the couch.

"Fine."

"I just want to make sure there are no ill effects since we have a stunt to do this morning."

"I'm fine and I apologize for jumping to conclusions this morning."

"Not necessary. I suppose I would have been just as suspicious under the circumstances. Have you always sleepwalked?"

"Not since I was a child."

"You don't remember anything?"

"I feel like the memory is just out of my reach. The last thing I recall was going to bed. But apparently I didn't stay there."

"I just want you to know, about last night, I didn't feel anything, you know…"

She feared she did. "You really don't have to—"

"No, I do. It wasn't sexual. I just wanted to get you dry and warm and make sure you were all right. I wasn't turned on. I guess that's what I'm trying to say."

"Please. *Stop*." She felt her face heat.

He looked as flustered as she felt. "It's not that I don't think you're attractive. Or that I wouldn't like to—"

"Jud! Please. *I understand*."

He nodded, looking uncomfortable—something rare for him.

Faith got up to glance outside from behind the curtains. The breakfast crowd was dispersing as the sun rose up out of the prairie, bright and golden. She would be working today after all, since apparently the other thunderstorm the weatherman had called for was nowhere in sight.

As she started to drop the curtain back in place, she saw Nancy Davis headed in the direction of Jud's trailer with the call sheets for the day and groaned.

Dropping the curtain, Faith hightailed it down the hall, motioning to Jud, who just looked confused. An instant later there was a knock at the door. Jud answered it.

"Mornin'," Faith heard him say.

"Have you seen Faith Bailey?" Nancy asked without returning the greeting.

"As a matter of fact, she just stopped over for coffee," Jud said smoothly.

Faith stepped out, holding her coffee cup in both hands. "Good morning." She smiled at Nancy as she took her revised call sheet. Nancy didn't smile back, her eyes darting between her and Jud.

Faith let out a low curse as Jud closed the door. "She thinks we spent the night together."

Jud laughed. "We did."

"You know what I mean."

"So she thinks we spent all night making love," Jud said, his words soft and seductive as a caress. "It doesn't matter if she does."

Faith wasn't so sure about that. There was something about Nancy Davis that bothered her.

FIVE MINUTES before ten, Eve Bailey Jackson pulled up in front of motel. She sat for a moment, so relieved to see that the rental car was still there that she was trembling.

She'd slept some. Carter had beaten her home and she'd had to make up an excuse for being so late coming home.

"I wanted to spend time with Faith," she'd said. Not a lie exactly. "I'm worried about her. You heard about the accident on the set."

They talked about that for a while, then went to bed. Eve was glad when her husband pulled her close and began to make love to her. She lost herself in his touch, needing the escape from her thoughts, her fears, her worries about what Mary Ellen Small would tell her come morning. What if the woman changed her mind and left?

After their lovemaking, exhausted and content, Eve surprised herself by falling asleep.

This morning she hadn't had to come up with a plausible story for her need to be in town by ten. Carter had gone off to work. She'd watched him leave, feeling guilty for not telling him about Mary Ellen. But then she would have had to tell him everything, and she wasn't ready to do that yet.

She had to hear the whole story.

As she got out of her car and headed for the motel room door, Eve felt another stab of guilt at the thought of Bridger. She pushed the guilt aside. There would be time to tell him everything.

Knocking on the door, she realized that the truth about their parents might be a secret she would have to keep to protect him. She prayed that that wasn't the case, but she had a bad feeling as the door opened and she saw Mary Ellen's face.

THE RUMORS about Jud and Faith ran like a wildfire through the film encampment. Brooke overheard someone in props talking about it before breakfast. She tried not to let it bother her, since everyone grew quiet when she walked past.

They thought she and Jud were an item and that she was brokenhearted by this turn of events.

It made her furious. She knew what people were saying. That first Brooke had lost her job to the bitch and now the bitch was sleeping with Brooke's man.

"Good morning," Jud said, joining her. He sounded too damned cheerful for his own good.

She grunted in response.

"Is there a problem?" he asked.

"You tell me," she snapped.

"None. None at all," he said, meeting her gaze.

Faith showed up then from the makeup and costume trailers, apparently ready for her stunt. Brooke noticed the bandage on her temple. Makeup had tried to hide it behind her hair, but it was still visible up close. The camera wouldn't pick it up since there wouldn't be any close-ups.

Brooke shot a glance to Jud in question.

He shrugged and shot her one of his grins. She began to relax. Everything was fine. This woman couldn't come between the relationship that Brooke had with Jud. She felt better than she had all morning.

Faith Bailey was a nobody. After this film, she would melt back into obscurity. Jud would forget her just as he had all the other women. The only true bond between a man and woman was friendship. And hers and Jud's was stronger than any film affair, Brooke told herself as she watched Jud whisper something into Faith's ear.

"ARE YOU SURE you're up to this today?" Jud whispered to Faith.

"I'm fine," she said under her breath.

"I'm just worried about that knock you took on your head," he whispered, shifting his body so Brooke couldn't read his lips. He'd seen how intently she'd been watching the two of them. No doubt the rumor mill had been running full tilt all morning.

Faith turned so that they were facing each other, so close that he could smell the scent of his soap on her skin. "I can do this. I'm fine."

He shrugged and stepped back, knowing that Brooke probably wasn't the only one watching them. He couldn't have cared less about what people were saying. But Faith cared.

Jud wanted her mind on the stunt they were about to perform—not on what the crew was saying about the two of them.

"Then let's do it," he said and grinned, hoping to relax her. They'd run through this stunt several times, and Faith knew what to do.

Out of the corner of his eye, he saw Brooke's impatient expression. Everyone was standing by. He knew Zander would have another panic attack if this film were delayed any further.

"We're ready!" he called.

The scene would be shot primarily from behind them as they rode along on horseback through the tall grass side by side. When they reached the mark, she would make her horse rear. The rattlesnake would be added later digitally.

Her horse would take off. Jud would chase her down, the film crew racing along beside him. He would ride up up next to her horse and pull her over onto his horse, rein in and drop to the ground to take her into his arms.

They hadn't practiced anything, except the exchange from her horse to his and the dismount. Faith had been flawless.

"Ready," Zander echoed across the set.

As stunt coordinator, Jud called "action," and he and Faith started riding across the prairie at a leisurely pace.

He wished that was what they were doing at this moment. Just the two of them riding out across the prairie with no cameras tracking their every move along with a half-dozen members of the film crew.

He tried to concentrate, but he kept thinking about how he'd felt waking up next to her this morning. He hadn't wanted her to wake up just yet. He loved holding her, smelling her, feeling the warmth of her body next to his own. He'd wanted her there always, he thought as they rode along, the cameras rolling behind them. And just the thought scared the hell out of him.

They reached the mark. On cue, Faith reared her horse and took off at a gallop, leaning over the mount as if for dear life.

Jud went after her, his heart suddenly pounding as if this were real, as if Faith really were in trouble and if he didn't catch her he might lose her.

He never had such crazy thoughts before during stunts. It was from seeing her hurt and confused last night, from being afraid for her. He recalled the odd feeling he'd gotten last night at dinner with his family and Faith. She'd felt so right there. Almost as if she belonged.

He caught up to her and reached for her, pulling her over

onto his horse as he reined to a stop and dropped to the ground to take her in his arms, relieved to have the stunt over, to have her safe.

"Got it in one!"

He barely heard the director. His heart was thunder in his chest as he pulled Faith to him, holding her as if for dear life as he brushed her hair back from her face and their eyes met.

Zander yelled, "Keep rolling," but Jud didn't comprehend the words.

His mouth dropped to Faith's and he kissed her with a fervor like none he'd ever known—just as the script called for—only he was no hero and this was no longer fiction.

FAITH CAME OUT of the kiss slowly to the sound of applause. She'd completely forgotten about the film crew the moment Jud had pulled her into his arms and kissed her.

"Cut!"

She drew back now, startled to see all the people watching them, smiling and clapping. Even director Erik Zander was smiling—a miracle in itself.

"That's a wrap. Another storm's moving in. We're moving to the covered set for the saloon scene." Zander looked over at Faith. "Good job, Bailey." Then he turned and walked off before Faith could say "Thank you."

Her legs were wobbly, Jud's kiss making her more off balance than any bump on the head could do. Her face fired with embarrassment. She'd been so into the kiss she'd been oblivious of where they were or who was watching.

Now she felt confused, not sure why Jud had kissed her and realizing he'd probably done it because it was part of the script. Or maybe he'd thought that since everyone was already talking about them, he'd give them something to talk about.

They looked at each other. Jud appeared as awkward as she was, as if he regretted the spur-of-the-moment kiss.

"I should get changed," she said when it appeared neither of them wanted to talk about the kiss and that Brooke was nearby watching them.

"You aren't needed for the saloon shoot and aren't scheduled again until tomorrow," he said. "Are you going to hang around here or go home to your ranch?" He glanced past her to where Brooke was packing up the rest of the gear, distracted for a moment.

So it was business as usual? Faith cleared her throat, stalling, wishing Brooke would leave. She wanted to talk to Jud, to understand what that kiss had been about. But she didn't want to say anything in front of Brooke. She couldn't help feeling that the woman resented her for taking her place.

"I don't know yet."

He nodded. "Just be careful," he whispered.

So it was her *safety* he was worried about?

"Jud can lead your horse back," Brooke said to her. "You look pale. Ride with me in the pickup."

"That's a good idea," Jud said before Faith could argue.

Brooke brushed Faith's hair back as if to inspect the small bandage on her temple. "Whatever did you run into?"

"I was just being clumsy," Faith said.

Brooke met her gaze, as if to let her know she knew she was lying.

The last thing Faith wanted to do was ride back to camp with Brooke, but she didn't want to make a fuss, especially after Jud had put in his two cents. Faith figured he just didn't want to ride back to the set with her, just the two of them, after the kiss.

So she climbed into the passenger side of the pickup as

Brooke slid behind the wheel. Out the window, she took one last look at Jud, trying to read his expression and failing.

"Nice job," Brooke said. "You really seem to know what you're doing."

"Thanks," she replied, although she suspected Brooke wasn't referring to the stunt.

"CONSTANCE AND PAUL WERE living in a rambling old house north of town that smelled of cooked cabbage and desperation," Mary Ellen said, resuming her story. "I drove by the spot where it used to be yesterday. It's gone. The building razed. The earth barren."

As she had done the night before, she'd made coffee. Only this time she'd picked up some donuts at the local grocery. Eve had taken a cup of the hot coffee and nibbled at one of the donuts, just to have something to do.

"They had aged during those months. Paul was working at the local tire shop. His body had filled out, and had it not been for the haggard look in his eyes, he would have been even more handsome than when I'd known him. Constance was—" Mary Ellen's eyes filled with tears "—beautiful. The pregnancy, you know. It made her glow. And while she'd told our mother that her life had been a nightmare, her unhappiness didn't show on her. Oh, she cried, of course, and begged again for my forgiveness. She said the pregnancy had been hard on her and that she needed to go home, to be around Mother. All I saw was her selfishness. Even after everything she'd done to me, she was only thinking of herself." Mary Ellen smiled. "I was unable to see my own selfishness in wanting to keep her apart from our mother and the people we had both known at home."

"Surely those same people had noticed that both your sister and your fiancé had disappeared," Eve said.

"I concocted believable stories. Paul was smart, a promising student in high school. Everyone believed that he'd had a chance to go to college early. I was still wearing his ring, still pretending that we would be married the next summer. Mother and I had been making wedding plans when my sister had called her, destroying even that hope."

Eve shook her head. "You couldn't possibly have believed that—"

"That Paul would come back to me?" She laughed softly. "What else did I have to hope for? I told myself that he would realize his mistake. I planned to make him suffer the rest of his life when he came crawling back."

"But what about the babies?" Eve realized even as she said it that she knew what had happened to the babies. She and Bridger would end up being adopted.

"I didn't care what happened to their baby. I didn't know then that she carried twins. I fear that would have made me hate her even more."

Eve said nothing, waiting, thinking she already knew the end of the story. She couldn't have been more wrong.

THE FIRST THING Faith noticed when she entered her trailer was the overturned chair. She stared at it. What was it doing in the middle of the room? She recalled putting it against the door before she'd gone to bed. Obviously at some point, she'd moved it.

But she wouldn't have left it overturned in the middle of the floor unless she'd left the trailer in a hurry.

She stared at it. Had she really been sleepwalking? Maybe she'd knocked it over. But wouldn't the noise have awakened her?

"I'll make you some tea," Brooke said, coming in the trailer behind her.

Faith had just assumed Brooke would leave once she dropped her off. "That isn't necessary, really." She wanted to be left alone so she could try to remember last night. Brooke was distracting her.

"I have my own special blend." Brooke pulled a small bag from her pocket and stepped into the small kitchen.

That's when Faith noticed the small trash can next to the stove. It was empty. Where was the rag doll she'd thrown in it last night? Someone had come in and taken it.

Her heart began to pound wildly. Someone had been in her trailer—*again*. Even if she *had* been sleepwalking, she wouldn't have taken that doll out of the trash.

"Please, I really just want to change and rest," she said to Brooke, who had been searching for something to make tea in. The trailers had come stocked with everything a camper might need, including pots and pans.

"Didn't get much sleep last night, huh?"

"No. I don't mean to be rude, but I don't drink tea. Please."

Brooke appeared to be about to argue, but she must have changed her mind. She pocketed the special blend and with a tight smile said, "I was just trying to help."

Somehow Faith found that hard to believe. "Thank you. I appreciate your concern." She closed the door behind Brooke and locked it. Then she took a step toward her bedroom, the bed coming into view, and stopped again.

The doll sat on the unmade bed, back to her pillow, dark eyes staring down the hallway at her.

It was just a doll. She knew that rationally. But still it sent her heart galloping. The doll on her bed meant someone had come into her trailer last night after she left.

Left for where?

Gingerly she peeled off the bandage and stepped into

the bathroom to stare into the mirror. There was a small cut, a bruised bump. What had she stumbled into?

As she touched her sore temple, she had a flash of memory. Her pulse quickened. The memory skidded away but not before she'd had a glimpse of walking past one of the trailers—the equipment trailer.

She'd been following something into the darkness. Following *someone*.

Chapter Eleven

Faith quickly showered and changed clothes, her mind racing. What had happened last night? Had she ended up confused with a knot on her head because she'd followed the person she'd seen?

There was only one way to know for sure. Dressed in her usual jeans, boots, snap-shirt and Western straw hat, she left her trailer and headed for the back of the equipment trailer.

The camp felt empty. Everyone must have gone to the saloon shoot. She concentrated on last night as she crossed the circle between the trailers. While her memory was still fuzzy, she felt as if she were retracing her footsteps.

But why would she come out into the night barefoot in only a nightgown? What had she seen? Something that had forced her not to take the time to change clothes or at least pull on her boots. It wouldn't have been the first time she'd acted impulsively. Or the last, she thought, as she neared the back of the equipment trailer.

Still, it bothered her that if she'd seen something that had made her rush out of her trailer like that; why hadn't she tried to get help? True, it wasn't in her nature to ask for help. She was mule-headed and probably thought she was more capable of taking care of herself than she was.

The cut and bump on her head—case in point.

At the back of the equipment trailer, she stared down at the ground. Was her memory playing tricks on her? She'd vaguely recalled following tracks.

What tracks there might have been had been washed away by the *storm* that had blown in later in the night apparently. The top surface of the ground had dried from the morning sun and the breeze that now stirred her hair.

She looked out over the prairie. From a distance the land in this part of Montana appeared flat. Just a huge expanse of grass that ran to the Little Rockies.

It was deceptive, because once you started across the land, you quickly realized it was anything but flat. The terrain rose and fell with gullies and rocky outcroppings. Antelope often appeared on the horizon only to disappear as if by magic when all they did was drop over a rise.

Faith headed in the direction she believed she'd gone last night. She kept getting snatches of memory, the strongest one of being cold and wet and scared. As she walked, she recalled the darkness and something over a rise. A light.

With a start she remembered the pickup parked against the embankment. Last night came back in a rush. The clank of a tailgate being dropped. The tracks in the muddy earth. She'd seen someone dragging what had looked like a body.

Her pulse raced at the thought. It had to have been a dream. If someone was missing from camp, surely by now it would have been noticed. She stopped to glance back. She could just make out the tops of the trailers in the distance. A few more steps and they would disappear entirely.

She shuddered at the realization that no one knew where she'd gone. No one would miss her. Was it possible that she really had seen someone dragging a body out to a truck somewhere near here? If so, that person might not have been missed yet.

Wishing now that she'd told someone where she was going, she dropped over the rise. Ahead she saw what looked like a dry creek bed. She recalled the feel of those rocks on her bare feet. She had to be getting close.

Edging to the top of the next rise, she peered over, half expecting to see the pickup parked where it had been last night. There was nothing in the dry creek bed. No pickup. No body.

She stood looking down. The rain had washed away any boot or drag marks in the earth, but it hadn't been able to wash away truck tracks.

Dropping down the small rise into the creek bed, Faith found where the pickup had been parked against the embankment. She remembered sneaking up to the truck to look into the back, but after that nothing until the memory of being wet and cold and stumbling back toward camp.

Had she seen the body in the bed of the truck? Or had she been hit on the head before she could?

She jumped as a large hand cupped her shoulder, and she swung around ready to put up a fight this time.

"Hey! Easy!" Jud said, taking a step back. "I didn't mean to scare you. Didn't you hear me? I was calling to you." His look said he was worried.

"I remember what happened last night."

"You remembered your nightmare?"

She shook her head. "I wasn't sleepwalking. I saw someone dragging a large, heavy object into the prairie. I remember thinking I didn't have time to dress."

Jud looked skeptical. "A large object?"

"I followed the person as far as the edge of camp. From there I followed the drag marks in the mud. The person was dragging a body, I'm sure of it."

"A body?"

"Look, you can see where a truck was parked against the embankment. Because the body was too heavy for the person to lift into the back of the pickup." She pointed at the tracks in the earth, then glanced at him and saw his expression. "Don't give me that look. I know what I saw."

"Someone dragging a body away from the camp," he repeated. "And you know it was a body because you saw this dead person?"

"Maybe. I remember sneaking up to the back of the pickup and either looking in the bed or starting to when I must have been hit. That explains the cut and bump on my temple and why when you found me I was confused."

"So you didn't see the body."

Her impatience went straight to anger. "I'm telling you what happened last night. The tracks prove it. There was a pickup parked right there. One of the crew trucks. The dome light was on, the tailgate down. It wasn't a dream, and I wasn't sleepwalking."

"Okay." He held up both hands. "Then we should get back to camp and find out who's missing."

Her relief at his words was at war with the feeling that he was just humoring her. It was as if he were counting on no one being missing from the set.

Just as he seemed to be counting on her forgetting about their earlier kiss.

JUD WASN'T SURE what scared him the most. Faith's conviction that she'd seen someone dragging a body to the dry creek bed last night or this overwhelming need of his to protect this woman.

As they walked back to the camp, neither speaking, he prayed she was wrong. Not because he wanted her to be wrong about anything. But if what she was saying were true, then she'd been in terrible danger last night.

And was still in danger.

She had to have been sleepwalking, and all of this was just part of a nightmare that had seemed so real that... that there were tracks from the pickup she swore she'd seen?

"Let me see what I can find out," he told her as they reached the edge of the camp. "Nancy will know since it's her job to keep track of everyone." He called her on his cell.

Nancy answered impatiently on the second ring.

"When you handed out the call sheets this morning, was anyone missing?"

"No. And you'd better not be missing for your stunt this morning." She hung up on him.

Jud thought about what Faith had asked him. *How well did he know Nancy?* Did *anyone* know Nancy? He'd gotten few impressions about her, except for one. He thought she had a crush on director Erik Zander.

Not that Zander would have noticed. He was at least twice her age. Not usually a problem for him, but she wasn't his type. While Nancy wasn't bad looking, she came off as frumpy. Odd, he thought, since that impression came only from the way she wore her hair and dressed. Her face, when not hidden behind her mousy brown hair, was quite pretty, and her figure, if not curvaceous, was slim. She would have definitely been Zander's type, if she'd dressed more provocatively. Odd that she hadn't figured that out.

"You said you didn't get to Whitehorse in time to do what you'd planned," Eve reminded Mary Ellen. The wind had kicked up outside the motel room. Another thunderstorm was on the way. The motel room felt too small already.

The older woman nodded. "I had just gotten to their little dreary house in the country when Constance went into labor. She pleaded with me to take her to the hospital. Paul had the car at work. Constance wasn't due for weeks."

"You didn't take her to the hospital," Eve said, knowing that was the only way she and her brother could have come into the world and been adopted illegally through the Whitehorse Sewing Circle.

For years the sewing circle had handled adoptions undercover, so to speak. They would find good homes for the babies and make each a baby quilt. It wasn't until recently that Eve had found out just how important that baby quilt was.

"No, I didn't take her to the hospital." Mary Ellen said it with a finality, and for the first time, Eve saw how much these decisions had plagued her life ever since. "I let my sister suffer, watched her cry and scream as she brought not one but two babies into the world."

"You must have helped her," Eve said.

"There was a point where I regretted what I'd done, but by then it was too late. We couldn't have reached the hospital in time. I was young. I knew nothing of babies and birth. I wrapped each baby in an old towel. I was scared. I didn't know what to do." She looked up at Eve. "You and your brother were so small, so fragile looking. As much as I hated my sister and Paul, I wanted you and your brother to live."

Eve listened as Mary Ellen told of her decision to take the babies to town. "Constance was too weak to travel. She insisted I just get the babies to the hospital. All she cared about was her babies. She loved you so much." The older woman's voice broke. "It was winter. I hadn't realized it, but a storm had blown in. I didn't get far before I got stuck in a drift. I saw a farmhouse and, taking the babies, I waded through the snow to it."

"I know we were flown to Whitehorse in a small plane two days later, so I assume we never made it to the hospital."

Mary Ellen shook her head. "I told the elderly woman that a runaway girl I'd come across had given birth to the babies and didn't want them. The woman said not to worry, she knew what to do. The storm got worse, though. I ended up being trapped there for two days."

Eve held her breath, knowing the story was about to end—and end badly. "My mother?" she asked, for the first time saying the words.

"When I found her, she had bled to death."

"SOMEONE *HAS* TO BE MISSING," Faith argued when Jud gave her the news.

"I talked to Nancy. Everyone is accounted for. Look, I don't like leaving you, but I have to get into town for the saloon shoot. Are you sure you're going to be all right? Why don't you come along?"

She shook her head stubbornly. She knew what she'd seen. "Then something large must be missing. If it wasn't a body, then it must have been equipment."

"Nothing appears to be missing," he repeated.

"How do you explain the pickup tracks in the dry creek bed then?"

"Maybe there was a pickup there last night. There are always lookie-loos around a movie set. Please come with me. I don't like leaving you here alone."

She met his gaze. His concern touched her even though she didn't want it to. "You'd better get going. I'll stop by after your shoot. Right now I just need some rest. Don't worry, I'll lock myself in."

His relief was almost palpable. "We'll figure this out, okay? Fortunately, no matter what happened last night, you came out of it just a little worse for wear."

She touched the knot on her temple under her bandage.

"So no real harm was done," he said.

Except for whoever that was who was dragged from the movie set, she thought, but she had the good sense to keep her mouth shut. No one was missing. She couldn't have seen a body being dragged away. Too bad she didn't believe that.

Jud seemed to think that was end of it. He didn't know her, she thought, as he waited until she'd locked the trailer door behind her before he headed for his pickup and Whitehorse.

Finding out how her mother had died, Eve began to cry even though she'd promised herself she wouldn't. Hadn't she known this was the case? Hadn't she known the moment Mary Ellen, instead of her mother, had contacted her?

"And Paul?" Eve asked after a moment.

Mary Ellen went very still. While her gaze appeared to be on the far motel wall, Eve knew it was in the past, thirty-four years ago in some run-down old house north of Whitehorse in the middle of winter.

"In my rush to get the babies to safety, I'd left my father's gun behind. I discovered Paul beside Constance's bed on the floor. Apparently he'd found her and seen the gun and…" She swallowed and looked away. "And thinking the babies lost as well, killed himself. Until that moment, I'd told myself that it was me he truly loved, not my sister."

Eve took a breath and let it out slowly. She knew she should hate this woman. How different hers and Bridger's lives would have been had Mary Ellen Small never lived. This hateful woman had destroyed two lives and changed Eve's and her brother's forever. They would never know their mother or father because of a sister's jealousy and revenge.

"Constance loved you and your brother more than her own life," Mary Ellen said, her hands now folded in her lap. "I have no doubt your father loved you equally as much or he wouldn't have done what he did."

"Where are they buried?" Eve asked.

"In the Whitehorse Cemetery in unmarked graves."

Eve nodded and rose slowly from the table. As a child she'd asked about the two white stones with no names on them.

"No one knows *who* they were," her mother had told her.

"But there are angels on the stones," Eve had said.

"Yes. I think they are both angels now."

Eve felt the full weight of the lies and truths she'd been told her whole life. Her mother had known who was buried in those graves. No doubt the Whitehorse Sewing Circle had purchased the headstones. They'd had to cover up the truth to protect Eve and Bridger.

How Eve wanted to expose them all. But exposing the Whitehorse Sewing Circle would mean exposing her own family. Her mother, her grandmother and grandfather had been some of the ringleaders of the illegal adoption faction. People Eve had known her whole life, good people, now elderly, had been involved. Even today, those people believed they were doing what was right for the babies by finding them homes all those years ago.

Their legacy was now in Eve's hands. She and her brother alone had been told by the sewing circle of the secrets that had been stitched into each quilt. Her own sisters were adopted. Who knew what their circumstances had been at birth? It was no wonder they said they had no desire to track down their birth parents.

But she feared there would be others who would show up one day in Whitehorse searching for the mother who gave them away, and Eve would have to decide whether or not to help them.

Eve looked at Mary Ellen. She didn't know what to say to this woman. Her *aunt*. Mary Ellen had saved hers and Bridger's lives. If she hadn't taken them to a neighbors...

And if she hadn't come to Whitehorse again and shared this painful story, Eve would have gone on looking into strangers' faces hoping to see her own.

"You understand now why I didn't want to tell you," Mary Ellen said without raising her head to look at Eve. "The shame and guilt is something I have carried alone all these years. Not even my own mother knows the truth. My father died believing that Constance simply ran away. I could never bear to tell them the truth, that they had lost one daughter because of the other."

What a terrible burden the woman had carried for thirty-four long years, Eve thought. "I'm glad you told me. I can see how hard it was for you. But if your sister told your mother everything when she called her—"

Mary Ellen shook her head. "All she told my mother was that she was in Whitehorse, Montana, and in terrible trouble and wanted to come home. I offered to go after her. I told my parents that when I got there, Constance was gone. I even offered to hire a private investigator to find her." She nodded. "I had become very good at lying."

Eve could see how those lies had crippled this woman. "You were so young when this happened—"

Mary Ellen swatted the words away. "There is no excuse for what I did. None."

"I'm sorry," Eve said. "I hope that by telling me you might be able to find some peace."

"I am in no place to ask you a favor," Mary Ellen said, her voice thick with emotion. "But I must. My mother, your *grandmother*, I want to tell her about you and your brother. She is innocent in all this. She is a wonderful woman who deserves to know she has two grandchildren."

"And a great-grandchild. Bridger's wife just had a baby boy. They named him Jack."

Mary Ellen's eyes flooded with tears. "It would mean everything to my mother, since I have never married."

A grandmother. A great-grandmother for Bridger's baby. Isn't this what Eve had always hoped for? Family? "I will have to talk to my brother first."

Mary Ellen nodded. "I understand. Please, let him know that my mother is nothing like me."

On impulse, Eve took the woman's hand. A woman who'd done despicable things and paid a high price all these years for them. "I will tell my brother that our mother died in childbirth and her babies were taken away to be given to good homes. That our father loved her so much and, thinking his children were also lost, took his own life. That is all he needs to know. It is time we all let go of the past."

Eve hugged her aunt for a long moment, then left, driving first to see her husband at the sheriff's office, desperately needing to be in his strong arms. Then to see her brother, Bridger.

JUD HAD TROUBLE concentrating. He hadn't been able to stop worrying about Faith. Fortunately he'd been in more than his fair share of fight scenes and could do them in his sleep. He was just glad when he was gone because he was anxious to find Faith. She'd said she would stop by, but she hadn't.

"Where the hell is Chantal?" Zander demanded when all of the stunts were completed and the saloon cleaned up for the interior shots.

Zander had rented the local bar for the day. According to the call sheet, Chantal and Nevada had three scenes to shoot before the day was over.

"I'll try to reach her," Nancy said, snapping open her cell phone. She listened for a few minutes, then left an urgent message. Cell phone coverage was sketchy in this part of the country, but more than likely Chantal just wasn't answering for whatever reason.

"She's probably on her way," Nancy said and gave Nevada a questioning glance.

"Don't look at *me*," he snapped. "I haven't seen her since…wait a minute." His face flushed. "I just remembered. Right before we all left, she said she had to run back to her trailer for something."

Zander swore profusely. "Nancy—"

"I'll go get her," Jud said. He wanted to check on Faith.

He told himself as he drove back out to the camp that she was fine. Probably she'd overslept. Or she could still be mad at him for not believing her about what she thought she'd seen last night and decided she didn't want to stop by.

As he topped the hill and saw the camp below, he felt a fresh wave of anxiety. He'd gotten Faith into this and now he feared that he'd put her in danger. Nearing the parking area, he saw that Faith's pickup was gone.

He felt a stab of disappointment. He'd hoped she was still sleeping. He wanted to see her, even if for only a few minutes.

Climbing out of his truck, he headed for Chantal's trailer, telling himself that Faith had probably gone to town just as she said she would. There was no cause for concern.

For whatever reason she hadn't stopped by to see him. No big deal. If it had been any other woman, he would have just shrugged it off.

"Grow up," he told himself as he tapped on Chantal's door. He could hear music coming from inside and wasn't surprised when she opened the door smelling of perfume and Scotch.

"I wondered how long it would take someone to realize I wasn't there," she said with a tight smile.

"Nevada just remembered that you'd gone back to your trailer for something."

Her face twisted in anger. "The bastard. I should have known. I told him to tell Nancy. That's the second damned time I've been stood up in two days." Her anger had quickly turned to self-pity. "Tell me, what am I doing wrong?" she asked with a come-hither look.

"I'm sure you're exaggerating," he said, waiting patiently for her, knowing Zander would be losing his mind waiting for her.

She pretended to pout. "I can understand Nevada forgetting me. The man's gorgeous and an idiot. But Keyes Hasting? I mean, the man is *old*. Not to mention ugly as a toad. And to make matters worse, it was *his* idea I meet him last night."

Jud hadn't been listening until then. "You were supposed to meet Keyes Hasting last night and he didn't show up? Is that what you're saying?"

"Yes, haven't you been listening to me?"

"Have you seen him since then?" he demanded.

"Are you serious? After he stood me up?"

Keyes Hasting. Had anyone seen him this morning? When Jud had asked Nancy if everyone was accounted for, she wouldn't have included Hasting.

Jud looked toward the parking area where Hasting's rental SUV had been parked yesterday. It was gone. Maybe he'd changed his mind about meeting with Chantal and had left. Or maybe he hadn't.

Either way, Jud now had to check Faith's trailer. It would probably be locked, and with her pickup gone, he knew rationally that she wouldn't be there. He knew he was probably wasting his time, but he had to try.

She'd been so convinced that she'd seen someone dragging a body away from camp. Why hadn't he listened to her?

He sprinted to the trailer anyway, knocked and tried the door, surprised and suddenly apprehensive to find it wasn't locked.

"Faith?" No answer. He stepped in. *"Faith?"*

Everything looked fine. No sign of a struggle. He glanced down the hall, feeling like a fool. It wasn't like him to panic like this. Or to feel this way about a woman he wasn't even dating—let alone sleeping with.

He was already turning toward the door to leave, when he saw the doll. It was propped up on the bed. He stepped toward it, noticing something strange.

When he was within a few feet of the bed, he saw that the doll had something on it just below the stitched eye. He picked up the doll. Was that dried blood on it?

Faith hadn't left this here. Someone must have put it there after she'd left. At least he hoped that was the case.

To scare her. Or warn her?

A sliver of worry burrowed under his skin at the thought that Brooke might resent Faith. Jealousy was an insidious thing. He'd seen it destroy people in this business.

"I thought we were in a big hurry to get me to the shoot?" Chantal called impatiently from the outside the trailer.

"Looks like there's another thunderstorm headed this way. Good thing we have a covered shoot this afternoon."

Jud grabbed the doll and stuffed it into his jacket pocket. The last thing he wanted was for Faith to see it. "Let's go," he said, closing the trailer door behind him. Zander would be having a fit.

But that was the least of Jud's worries as he headed for his pickup, dark clouds rolling in.

FAITH HAD LEFT the trailer, the doll on the bed, and driven to the rest home to see her grandmother, Nina Mae. No reason to throw the doll away again so it could show up in the same place again.

She and her sisters stopped by the rest home every day or so to see their grandmother, even though Nina Mae never recognized them anymore. Her grandmother on her mother's side had Alzheimer's. But Nina Mae was always glad to see Faith, even if she didn't have any idea who she was.

After that, Faith had driven out to the ranch, only to find Eve gone. At loose ends, Faith had started back to town just as it had begun to rain.

The rain and dark clouds did nothing to improve her mood. She was still upset with Jud for not believing her about last night. He didn't want to believe her, she thought, as her cell phone rang.

"Hello?" She was hoping it would be him. Now that he'd had time to think about it, he was calling to say he'd changed his mind. He believed her.

It wasn't Jud.

It was Sheriff Carter Jackson, her brother-in-law.

"I got that information you asked for on Erik Zander," Carter said.

She'd completely forgotten she'd asked him for it.

"That car accident twenty-three years ago?" Carter said. "Zander got a DUI and a ticket for leaving the scene of the accident, but he managed to skate on a manslaughter charge. The young woman with him was killed. He swore she was dead when he left the scene to get help, but he didn't call in the accident until two hours later, after he'd sobered up a little."

Faith felt sick. What if the woman had been alive those two hours? She knew people panicked and he'd been young twenty-three years ago, an up-and-coming director who'd already made a name for himself.

But two deaths both involving young women?

"I did discover something I thought you might find interesting," Carter was saying. "The dead woman went by Star Bishop, but her legal name was Angie Harris. She'd just gotten a divorce and moved to California. Her maiden name was Keifer, same as Brooke's before she changed it to Keith. According to birth records, Angie Kiefer gave birth to a daughter twenty-seven years ago. Samantha Brooke."

Brooke Keith was the daughter of the dead woman?

Chapter Twelve

Faith jumped at a tap on her pickup's side window. Her heart lodged in her throat as she looked over to find Brooke Keith staring in at her from the rain.

"I have to go," Faith said into the phone and snapped it shut as she whirred down the window. A gust of cold, wet air rushed in. Just the sight of Brooke standing there had already made her shiver. Now she felt chilled to the bone.

"Brooke." Frantically, Faith tried to remember what she'd been saying on the phone. Had Brooke overheard the conversation from outside the truck?

"I saw you sitting there," Brooke said, her demeanor odd, but probably no odder than usual. "I realized I came on a little too strong earlier. Sorry. It's wet out here. Could we talk in your pickup?"

Before Faith could react, Brooke ran around to the passenger side of the pickup. The door swung open and Brooke slid in, shaking off raindrops as she closed the door behind her.

Faith tried to hide how anxious it made her having Brooke Keith in the cab of her pickup.

What did she want? Clearly, the woman had something on her mind, and given what Brooke might have just overheard, that in itself was cause for concern.

Her instincts told her Brooke didn't like her as it was.

She tried not to think about what the sheriff had discovered. What did it mean, if anything? Hollywood was a small world, kind of like Montana in that everyone seemed related, even though in Montana's case, it was a big state.

Maybe it was no secret that Brooke was this dead woman's daughter. Maybe even Erik Zander was aware of it. Or maybe not.

Either way, could this explain the "accidents" that had been happening on the set?

"AM I MAKING YOU NERVOUS?" Brooke asked, amused. "You should have seen your face when I tapped on your window. You looked as if you'd seen a ghost."

"You just startled me, that's all," Faith said.

That wasn't all. Faith hadn't wanted her to get into the pickup. Just like back at the trailer when she'd turned down tea. Faith had been almost rude to her. And now she seemed more than nervous. She almost seemed scared.

Brooke remembered Faith's expression when she'd turned from the phone to the window to find her standing just outside. If only she'd been able to hear the phone conversation, but the rain on the pickup had been too noisy. She wondered who Faith had been talking to. Jud?

"You still seem nervous. Is it because I wanted to talk to you?" Brooke asked.

"I guess that depends on what you want to talk to me about," Faith said, her gaze wary.

"I wanted to talk to you about Jud."

"Jud?" Faith looked relieved.

What had Faith thought she wanted to talk to her about? The woman was smiling now, apparently relaxed.

"Look, if this is about last night…"

Brooke waved that off. "Jud gets romantically involved on every movie set."

Faith's eyes narrowed. "Really?"

"He's a good-looking guy. Even intelligent women fall for him. You're new to movie sets so I thought I should warn you. The affair always ends at the end of the movie." She shrugged. "It's just the way Jud is."

"Is that how it was with the two of you?"

Brooke was taken aback. "Jud and I never—" She caught herself. She'd let everyone think she and Jud had been lovers after a big spread in one of the stuntmen magazines. Jud hadn't cared, since it was a normal occurrence for him to be linked with one woman after another, true or not.

"Jud and I are friends. *Good* friends. It's a kind of bond no other woman has ever been able to break."

Faith nodded. She was too calm, taking this better than Brooke had expected. Probably because she thought she was different from all Jud's other lovers. She thought she would be the one who lasted. Maybe she was a bigger fool than Brooke thought.

The woman was headed for heartbreak and refused to believe it. Well, she'd been warned. Faith seemed like a nice enough person. Too bad she'd gotten caught up in something she could neither understand nor get out of at this point.

"It's good that Jud has a friend like you," Faith said, fidgeting with her keys.

Brooke couldn't tell if she was being sincere or facetious. "I'm glad you see it that way."

"What other way is there to see it?"

Brooke didn't know what else to say. "I just want you to know, that no matter what happens, it's nothing personal."

"I never thought it was." Faith smiled. "I'm glad you suggested this talk, because there's something I wanted to ask you."

Brooke braced herself, not sure why she needed to, just something in Faith's moment of hesitation before she leaned forward conspiratorially and asked, "Is there any chance that the accidents on the film set aren't accidents at all?"

MARY ELLEN PACKED UP her things at the motel. It shouldn't have taken much time, since she'd brought so little. But she was so exhausted and completely drained that doing anything took all her effort.

Had she done the wrong thing by telling Eve the truth? Eve's husband was the sheriff. Maybe she'd gone to him and any moment Mary Ellen would hear a knock at the door and she would be arrested.

But no knock came. Just another thunderstorm with lightning that flashed behind the curtains and thunder that rattled the windowpanes.

Eve had said she hoped this would bring Mary Ellen some peace, as if that were a possibility. She'd known telling the story to her sister's child would only bring it all back, every horrible, deplorable moment of it. And it had.

There could be no forgiveness. Not from her sister. Not from herself. What she'd done was monstrous. Her repentance had been a life cut off from the world, living simply, suffering alone.

She hadn't told Eve in the hope that she might be forgiven. She'd told the truth because she'd had to. She couldn't let Eve and her brother keep searching for their mother the way her parents had waited for years for Constance to come home.

No matter what Eve and her brother decided to do, Mary Ellen couldn't let her mother spend another day believing that Constance might come home again.

She hadn't told her parents because she'd believed that the truth would kill them. She'd been their perfect daughter, the one they'd always depended on.

After Constance left, her parents had leaned on her even more. "I don't know what we would do without you," they used to say. "We've lost Constance, but if we lost you, Mary Ellen…"

So she hadn't told them the truth, sparing them she told herself while saving herself from their reaction to what she'd done.

As she moved to the door with her suitcase, her cell phone rang. "Hello?" She expected it to be her mother. No matter what she planned to tell her, Mary Ellen wasn't going to tell her over the phone.

"Mary Ellen?" It was Eve.

She had to sit down on the motel bed. Her legs just didn't want to hold her. "Yes?"

"I've spoken to my brother. We want to meet our grandmother."

Mary Ellen began to cry, not softly, quietly, but big gulping sobs. When she could finally get herself under control, she said, "My mother will be so happy. I had already decided to tell her the truth when I got home."

"I don't think that's necessary," Eve said. "Maybe you should tell her what I told my brother. How Constance died giving birth, how the babies were adopted, believing Constance was a runaway, and how our father, finding his wife dead and babies gone, couldn't go on living."

Mary Ellen was silent for a long time. "What about the *truth?*"

"That is the truth," Eve said. "I hope your mother is well enough that the two of you can come to Montana so we can all get to know each other."

Again Mary Ellen couldn't speak for a long moment. "Thank you." Overwhelmed with emotion, she was unable to say more.

When she finally had control again, she loaded her suitcase in the rental car and headed south down the long two-lane highway. Pulling out her cell phone she keyed in her mother's number.

"Mary Ellen?" her mother said anxiously. "Is there something wrong, dear?"

"I'll tell you all about it when I get home from Montana, but I have good news, Mom." She could hear her mother sobbing softly on the other end of the line.

"Constance?"

Mary Ellen felt that pang she always felt. "I didn't want to tell you on the phone, but Constance died giving birth to twins. A son and a daughter. The daughter, Eve Bailey Jackson, looks just like Constance. I haven't seen the son yet. They're thirty-four years old. The son's wife recently gave birth to a baby boy. You're a great-grandmother."

FAITH SAW Brooke's reaction. Surprise, then something more wary.

"What are you talking about?"

"I think someone is purposely trying to sabotage the film," Faith said.

Brooke let out a short, rude laugh. "Why? This film is going to fail all by itself. Sorry to tell you this, but this flick will be lucky if it doesn't go straight to DVD. It's a dog. Bow wow."

"Then why would the director agree to make it? I

heard around the set that Erik Zander sunk everything he owned into it."

The stuntwoman shrugged. "Directors and producers make bad movies all the time. What else is he going to do?"

"Still, these so-called accidents—"

"You really are naive about the film industry, aren't you?" Brooke said, her smile laden with sarcasm. "It's a cheap film. We have a fourth of the crew we should have and our props look like they were built by third-graders. Of course there are going to be accidents."

"Like a rattlesnake crawling into your trailer?"

That stopped Brooke for a long moment. "That was more than likely personal. If you stay around this industry long enough, you make enemies. These people play rough."

"It almost killed you."

"What doesn't kill you makes you stronger, right?" Brooke chuckled and started to open the pickup door. "Remember what I said about Jud. In fact, I believe you have only one more stunt. I'd suggest you get off the set as quickly as possible when you're done with it tomorrow. You'll save yourself a lot of pain if you sever ties with Jud Corbett as fast as possible and don't look back."

Faith didn't get a chance to reply before Brooke opened the door and was gone. Which was probably just as well, considering what Faith might have said.

She watched Brooke head for one of the film's rented trucks parked across the street and thought about the truck she saw last night in the dry creek bed. It could have been the same pickup.

Faith had wanted to ask Brooke about her mother. She wasn't sure why she hadn't. Maybe she didn't want to tip her hand if it was a well-kept secret. Or maybe common sense had overruled.

Even if Brooke had admitted to being the daughter of Angie Keifer, that didn't mean she was behind the accidents on the set. Especially when she'd been the victim of the first accident and had almost died. Even though Brooke had tried to shrug it off, Faith suspected there was more to the story.

She started the engine to let the defroster clear the fogged windshield. She knew she should take both Nancy's and Brooke's advice and leave well enough alone.

If only that were in her nature.

As the windshield started to clear, Faith looked up and saw the dark shape of a person standing in front of the truck. For one heart-stopping moment, she thought it was Brooke again.

"Jud?" Faith asked, rolling down her window partway as he came around to her door.

"We need to talk," he said, and she motioned him around to the passenger side of the car and out of the rain.

Jud slid in, closing the door to the rain and cold, bringing with him his scent of leather and the outdoors. Suddenly the pickup cab felt too confined, too intimate. Her heart kicked up a beat and she was reminded of being in his arms earlier and that blamed kiss.

"What are you doing?" he demanded.

She stared at him in confusion. "What?"

"I just ran into Brooke. She said you talked to her about the accidents on the set. Now she's worried you won't be able to do your job, and I wouldn't be surprised if she goes to the director with this."

"So you're worried that I might lose my job?" He seemed awfully upset about it. Because he'd gotten her the job to start with? "Look, if you're worried that it might reflect on you since you're the one who suggested me—"

"Hell, no. I'm not thinking about my damned job. I'm

worried about you. If we're right about someone purposely causing these incidents, then you've just made yourself a target. And after what happened to you last night, getting fired might be the best thing that could happen to you."

All she heard was the "we're" part. "So you agree with me?"

"That's beside the point," he snapped, pulling off his Stetson to run his fingers through his hair. He had beautiful hair—and fingers, and Faith found herself momentarily distracted by both.

"Brooke was the one who insisted she had to talk to me."

He frowned. "Not about the accidents?"

"No. About *you*."

That shut him up. "Me?"

"She wanted to warn me about you. She said you had affairs on all the sets and broke them off at the end of the movie, leaving a trail of women behind. She swears you will break my heart just as you have all the others. Thanks to you, she thinks we're lovers."

"First off, I don't date women I work with. It's the Corbett Code. Dinner with the family the other night was *not* a date. I didn't kiss you when I took you back to your trailer, did I?"

"Nope. But you wanted to."

He smiled at that. "Oh, I wanted to do a lot more than that."

She felt her face heat up, thinking their minds that night had been on the same fast track. Good thing neither of them had acted on it.

"Second, I make no promises to the women I date, and believe me, I have left few broken hearts and dated many less women than my reputation would indicate.

"Third—" his gaze locked with hers across the close expanse of the pickup's cab "—I should never have gotten you into this."

She reached over and pressed a finger to his lips. "You gave me my heart's desire."

At his grin, she quickly removed her finger, realizing too late what she'd said.

"Is that your *only* heart's desire?" he asked softly.

She felt heat rush up from her toes, toes now curling in her boots. This was why Jud Corbett had such a way with women. She held up her hands as if that act alone could ward him off—let alone save her from the way he made her feel.

He took both her hands in his large ones and dragged her to him. The kiss on the set had been passionate enough but impulsive.

But there was nothing impulsive about this kiss. This was one of those I've-wanted-to-do-this-since-the-first-time-I-saw-you kisses. A saved-up, thought-out, dreamed-of and passionately yearned-for kiss.

She felt herself melt into his arms, his mouth warm, his lips strong and sure. It swept her up like an adventure where anything was possible.

Jud pulled her closer, melding their bodies together, as he explored her mouth, his hands tangled in her hair, his body hard and possessive.

When he finally let her come up for air, she was breathing hard, heart racing, traitorous body crying out for more. The pickup's windows were steamed over even though the engine was still running, the heater working as hard as it could to clear the glass.

The outside world appeared to be lost, which was just fine with her. She never wanted to leave this pickup cab or this man's arms.

Rational thought and reality came back slowly. She heard a car drive by, splashing through a puddle. A car door slammed nearby. The blast of the afternoon passenger train whistle as it approached the depot across the tracks from downtown. Brooke's warning, true or not.

"No, oh no," Faith whispered, her voice a croak as she pulled away. What had she been thinking? Even if half the stories about him were lies, there was that other half. She knew all about this man and his women. She wasn't about to become another notch on his six-shooter.

Jud looked surprisingly as shaken as she felt. "Wow. That was—"

"Wrong," she said, finally finding her voice. "What happened to that Corbett Code of yours?" she demanded, angry with him, even angrier with herself for enjoying every nanosecond locked in his kiss.

"To hell with the code. This is different. What I feel with you…what I felt from the first time I laid eyes on you. This is—" He was looking into her eyes, searching for what?

Her to fall for his line? "You say that to every woman." *Tell me it isn't true! Deny it, damn you!*

"You don't believe that. You feel this, too." He frowned, looking suddenly unsure of himself. "Am I wrong?"

She wanted to lie. For her own protection. Jud Corbett scared her. These feelings scared her. She'd never felt anything like what she'd experienced with him from the moment she saw him leaning on the jack fence watching her do her stunts.

"Faith, look at me." He reached over and lifted her chin with his warm fingers. "Tell me you didn't feel anything and I will get out of this pickup right now and never touch you again."

The lie caught in her throat at the thought of never feeling his touch, his lips, his arms around her again.

"That's what I thought." His relief surprised her. He laughed softly, leaned back, sighing as their gazes met.

"This scares me as much as it does you, maybe more, and if I did 'date' women I worked with while on a movie, as Brooke said, then I would be making love to you right now, right here, on Whitehorse, Montana's, main street."

"You sure about that?" she teased.

He grinned. "Yeah, and you'd let me." His expression sobered. "I was looking for you for another reason, actually. Isn't your brother-in-law the sheriff?"

"Yes, why?"

"I think we should go talk to him about what you saw last night."

Faith was feeling so many things right at that moment, relief and a whole new wave of tenderness toward this man. "You *believe* me?" She couldn't help grinning. "What changed your mind?"

"Keyes Hasting. Apparently he'd planned to meet Chantal last night but didn't show."

"Hasting? That older man I saw on the set yesterday?"

Jud nodded. "He invests in films occasionally and apparently has mob connections."

"You think he invested in *Death at Lost Creek?*"

"Seems likely, since he showed up," Jud said, frowning. "The word on the street was that Zander tied up every cent he had in the film. But it could be that wasn't enough and he went to Hasting. Either way, I think we'd better find out if Keyes Hasting is missing."

SHERIFF CARTER JACKSON listened as Faith told him what she'd seen the night before. He frowned as she related the part about being struck and wandering back into camp dazed.

"Why didn't you come to me with this sooner?" Carter demanded when she'd finished. "You might have mentioned it earlier when we talked."

"That's my fault," Jud spoke up. "No one was missing from the set this morning, and I was convinced Faith had been sleepwalking." He looked chagrined. "Also, I didn't want to believe it. I'd hoped to get through with the film before there was any more trouble."

Carter motioned for them to wait as he made a few calls. As he finished the last call, he hung up and looked at the two of them.

"Hasting hasn't used his plane ticket back to California," the sheriff said. "Nor has he turned in his rental car, and his family hasn't heard from him since yesterday, but they said he was planning to fly back this afternoon from Billings."

Faith shuddered. Like Jud, she also hadn't wanted to believe it was a body that she'd seen dragged away from the set.

"I don't want you going back out there until I get to the bottom of this," Carter said.

"I have a stunt tomorrow, my last," Faith said.

The sheriff swore. "At least don't stay out there at night."

"I'll stay at the ranch tonight," Faith told him.

"I'll make sure she's safe," Jud said. "I don't think she should be alone."

Faith couldn't believe they were talking about her as if she wasn't in the room. "Excuse me. I have some say in this."

"No," Jud said. "If what you saw last night was someone dragging off Hasting's body and they got close enough to you to smack you in the head, then no, you don't have any say. They will be worried that you can recognize them."

Faith started to argue, but Carter said, "Jud's right. That's exactly what I'm worried about. I don't want you staying alone. Eve will want—"

Faith was just about to say she didn't want Carter bothering Eve with this when Jud spoke up. "I'll stay with

Faith. We have a stunt we need to go over, anyway. I won't let her out of my sight."

Faith wanted to object, but this was better than having Eve worrying over her. "So that's settled. Now, are you both happy?" She rose to leave.

"I need to talk to the sheriff for just a minute," Jud said. "Why don't we just take one rig to your ranch? I can bring you back to your pickup in the morning." He started to hand Faith his keys.

"I'll wait for you in *my* truck," she said. She'd always been independent, capable of taking care of herself, and she wasn't about to give that up now when she felt she needed it the most.

If her life was in jeopardy because of what she'd seen last night, then she needed more than ever to keep her wits about her. She'd never liked the fairy tales where the handsome prince saved the princess. She wanted to be the princess who's able to save herself.

Jud had cast himself in the role as her protector. But it was a temporary role, and she wasn't about to kid herself that she could depend on him to always be around when she needed him. Their feelings for each other aside, he would be off to another film after this one. And she...well, she would be staying on the ranch until fall, and then who knew what she would do.

Not that it mattered. In a few days, the movie would be over and that would be the last she saw of Jud Corbett.

JUD WAITED until he saw Faith cross the street to her pickup. "Mule-headed, isn't she?" he said with a grin.

"Runs in the family," the sheriff agreed. "All three Bailey girls are like that. More spirit than common sense."

Jud turned his attention from the window back to the

sheriff. "Don't worry about her. I won't let anything happen to her."

"I appreciate that, but I'm still going to have a deputy near the ranch tonight to keep an eye on things," Carter said. "I didn't want to say anything to Faith because I know what her reaction would be."

Jud nodded. He could well imagine. "Faith's scared but she doesn't want to admit it. Nor does she want to believe that she can't take care of herself. It's one of the things I love about her."

Carter gaze sharpened at the word *love*. "I'm very fond of my sister-in-law."

"So am I." Jud reached into his pocket. "I didn't want her to see this," he said as he reached into his pocket and pulled out the small rag doll he'd found on Faith's bed. "I found it in her trailer where someone had left it. Everyone who's had an 'accident' found one of these beforehand."

Carter took the doll with obvious reluctance. "Are these props for the film?"

"No, these are much cruder made, much uglier. No one seems to know where they came from."

"What's this on the doll?" the sheriff asked.

"That's why I wanted you to see it," Jud said. "I think it's a drop of blood."

Chapter Thirteen

"Why did you want to see my brother-in-law alone?" Faith asked once they were on the road south toward the Bailey Ranch.

"I just wanted to reassure him that I wouldn't let anything happen to you."

"I can take care of myself."

"I know." She could feel his gaze on her. "You're the strongest woman I think I've ever met. And the most stubborn."

"Thank you," she said, and Jud laughed as his gaze took in the country sprawled ahead of them. The land ran south in rolling hills of green to fan out in ridges and deep ravines before falling to the river bottom.

The Missouri cut a deep gorge through the land as it twisted its way east before joining the Mississippi to run to the Gulf of Mexico.

Another thunderstorm had blown through. A breeze swept out the dark clouds, leaving behind a crystalline canopy of blue stretched over their heads from horizon to horizon. The sun hung over the Bear Paw and Little Rocky mountains, painting the scene before them in dramatic golden light.

It had turned into one of those breathtaking Montana

afternoons and having Jud Corbett sitting just inches away only intensified the experience.

Faith put down her window partway and breathed in the fresh air. It smelled of rain and grass and promise—and helped cool down her thoughts. She was angry and scared and swamped with emotions she didn't want to be feeling for the man beside her. And now they were driving out to her family ranch for the night. Just the two of them in that big house where she'd grown up.

"You all right?" Jud asked.

"No." She wondered if she would ever be all right again. For sure she would measure every man she met from this moment on against Jud Corbett, and they would come up lacking.

"You can talk to me," he said quietly.

She laughed at that. Talking was the last thing she wanted to do with him.

Suddenly she hit the brakes and brought the pickup to a skidding stop.

"What the—"

Before Jud could finish, she pulled off the road, dropping down into a gully filled with stunted aspens. The leaves rattled in the breeze. Rain droplets on each leaf caught the last of the day's light and sent it back in jeweled prisms.

She brought the pickup to a stop in the stand of aspens and, shutting off the motor, turned in the seat to glare at Jud. "I have to live life on my terms."

He nodded, looking concerned that she'd lost her mind.

She smiled ruefully. "You think I'm crazy. Well, welcome to the club. I think I must be certifiable but even that will be on my terms."

Faith unlatched her seat belt and leaned toward him to brush her lips over his. He froze as if unsure of what was going on. This time, she kissed him softly and pulled back to gaze into his eyes. "Make love to me."

His gaze locked with hers. *"Here? Now?"*

Her smile broadened. "Here. Now."

"And you're sure you want this as much as I do?" he asked, teasing now.

Body, heart and soul. Her rational mind put up a good fight but was out numbered. Faith wanted him, come hell or high water. If this was a mistake, then she was willing to live with it. She was through putting up a fight. She didn't try to make more of this than it was. They wanted each other desperately. Tomorrow she could deal with regrets and recriminations, but today she would give herself freely, surrender to Jud Corbett in a way she'd never surrendered to any man before.

"I want it *more* than you do," she teased back.

He laughed. "Not a chance," he said as he unsnapped his seat belt and dragged her into his arms. His mouth took possession of hers, stealing her breath.

She heard his sharp intake of breath as he peeled off her blouse, his gaze on her rounded breasts, the nipples hard as stones and pressing into the lacy fabric.

He cupped her breasts in his large hands, his thumbs feathering the already aching nipples and making her groan with longing. She dragged off his shirt to bare his muscular chest and the dark fuzz of hair that fell in a V to the waist of his jeans.

She pressed her hands to the warm flesh. His mouth dropped to the points of her breasts. Her head lolled back, mouth open, a sound coming out of her that she'd never heard before.

He shoved her back against the seat. Her body came alive under his lips, his fingers, his body.

Frantically, she fumbled at his Western belt, then the zipper on his jeans. She felt her jeans tugged down, heard her panties tear, and then his fingers were on her, in her, and she was gasping as he entered her.

Locked together in the ancient rhythm of lovemaking, the pickup rocking, Faith soared to new, rare heights until like a roller-coaster ride that has climbed to its highest point ever, she fell over the edge. Weightless and yet every nerve ending infinitely acute, she clung to Jud until their shared shudders of pleasure ebbed away like the last of the day's light.

He held her until their breathing slowed and heartbeats resumed their normal speed, then they untangled themselves, laughing in the small confines of the pickup's cab.

"That isn't the way I wanted our first time together," he said as he cupped her face in his hands and kissed her tenderly.

She smiled, trying to imagine their first time being any other way as they sorted through their clothing and stepped out into the evening air to finish dressing.

When they got back into the truck, a quiet settled between them. She could hear the soft sound of his breathing and remembered the steady, sure beat of his heart against her breast.

ERIK ZANDER HADN'T realized what an aversion he had to the sight of a police car until the sheriff's car pulled up on the set.

The sheriff was young, and handsome enough that he could have been in movies. "Sheriff," Zander said, shaking his hand. "I'm Erik Zander, the director here."

"Mr. Zander. Is there somewhere we could have a few words?"

"Sure, let's go to my trailer. But please, call me Zander, everyone does." He walked toward the circle of RVs, studying the sheriff out of the corner of his eye. For days he'd been waiting for the other shoe to drop, unable to sleep, unable to get drunk, unable to enjoy the only thing he ever enjoyed—his Scotch.

Now he wondered if this was the other shoe about to drop.

"Have you ever thought about getting into the movies?" Zander asked the sheriff as they neared the trailer. "I could definitely get you a screen test."

"Thanks, but I'll pass."

Zander reached the trailer and held the door open for the lawman, more worried than ever. What man in his right mind would pass up a chance to be in a movie?

"Can I offer you a drink?" he asked, following the sheriff inside.

"No, thank you. If we could just sit down…"

Zander could feel the sheriff watching him closely and wished he wasn't so nervous. He offered the lawman the couch and he took the recliner. "So, what's up?"

"I wanted to ask you about Mr. Keyes Hasting."

Zander blinked. "Hasting?" He felt him stomach roil. "Why? Has something happened to him?"

The sheriff looked up as he pulled out a tape recorder and set it on the end table between them. "Why would you ask that?"

"Because you're here asking questions about him." Zander would have killed for a drink. Anything to steady his nerves.

"When was the last time you saw him?"

"Day before yesterday, I guess."

"Mr. Hasting came out here?"

Zander nodded. "He wanted a tour of the set. I gave him one and, as far as I knew, he left."

"You didn't see him leave?"

"No, I was busy trying to get this film finished."

"Mr. Hasting seems to be missing," the sheriff said.

"Missing?"

"Is there anyone who might want to harm Mr. Hasting?"

Zander laughed. "The mob. Anyone who's done business with him. Or met him."

The sheriff wasn't amused. "Have you done business with him?"

"Hell, no. You couldn't get me to borrow money from that man." He realized he was talking too much. Something about a uniform and a badge made him nervous. Could be those other times he'd been questioned and expected to be arrested. "The last person you want to be in debt to is Keyes Hasting."

"Why is that?"

Zander shrugged. "Because the guy is a bastard and plays for keeps. If you owe him money and don't pay, you could get your legs broken or end up in the river wearing cement slippers."

"Was someone on the set in debt to him?"

The question took Zander by surprise. He hadn't considered that. But now that he thought about it, he wasn't sure Hasting had come here to see him. He'd just assumed Hasting had been his benefactor, the person behind this film.

But Hasting hadn't seemed interested in seeing the set or the dailies. He'd seemed distracted.

"Mr. Zander?"

He blinked. "Sorry. I was thinking. I don't know if anyone was in debt to him." He tried to remember who he'd seen Hasting talking to yesterday.

FAITH DROVE the rest of the way to the ranch with the window down. The evening was a rare one in so many ways, she thought, as she parked in front of the ranch house.

"It's just as I pictured it," Jud said, smiling over at her.

She loved this house, with its white clapboard siding, the sprawling front porch, the old windowpanes that looked out over the ranch.

They were barely through the front door before she was in his arms again. "This time we do it my way," Jud said, grinning and sweeping her up into his arms. "Your room at the top of the stairs?"

"First one on the right," she said, laughing as he carried her up the stairs without even breathing hard and lowered her to her bed.

He made love to her slowly, making her cry out with pleasure again and again until she lay spent in his arms.

Sated, they lay spooned together, his heartbeat in sync with her own, his breath a warm assurance on her neck as darkness crept in, covering them like a warm blanket.

JUD WOKE to warmth and a sensation for being both content and complete. He lay perfectly still, not wanting to lose that sensation. Faith lay curled next to him, her warm backside snuggled against him, his arm around her, their hands clasped.

He couldn't remember ever waking up with a woman holding his hand. There was something tender about it. Nor could he remember feeling so happy. Dangerous feelings for a man who wasn't interested in anything long term.

And yet he didn't move, didn't want this moment to end. He felt Faith stir. She let out a contented sigh and pressed against him, her hand squeezing his as she brought it closer to her lips.

Jud closed his eyes, fighting the feelings this woman evoked in him. Yesterday and last night were like a dream he never wanted to end. Their lovemaking had been so…natural, as if they could do it every day until the day they died.

Crazy, he knew, but he'd never felt so close to a woman before. The thought of never holding her again was like a blade to his heart. For the first time in his life, he wasn't looking forward to moving on.

FAITH WOKE with a start. For a moment she couldn't remember where she was. Her gaze took in the room she'd grown up in, but other than that, this was unfamiliar territory. She'd never made love with a man in this house, in this bed, in this manner. She'd never given herself so completely, felt so safe, knowing all the time that this was temporary.

She let go of Jud's hand and rolled over to face him. He was even more handsome in the morning looking a little sleepy, a little vulnerable. She couldn't help but smile as she touched her fingers to his rough unshaven jaw.

Her cell phone rang. She glanced at the clock. It was early. The sun had just come up. They weren't expected on the set for hours yet.

"Hello?" She had expected her sister to call last night and check on her. Or at least Carter to call. Neither had, and now that she thought about it, that was odd.

As she answered the phone, she swung out of bed and pulled Jud's shirt on as she stepped to the second-story window. A sheriff's deputy's car was parked in the trees not far from the house.

"Faith." Carter's voice startled her.

"You had a deputy watching the house all night?" she snapped angrily.

"I do what I have to do to protect my family and this community," he said, sounding irritated. "I called because Keyes Hasting has been found."

Her heart flip-flopped. If it wasn't Hasting she'd seen being dragged away from the set—

"He was found murdered in his rental car not far from Lost Creek ghost town."

"Oh, no." Behind her, Jud looked concerned.

"Erik Zander has been taken into custody. I want you to stay put. The assistant director, Nancy Davis, said she will let you and Jud know as to plans regarding finishing the film."

Faith flashed on the memory. Someone dragging away what had looked like a body. It had been Zander?

"Zander confessed?"

Another short silence. "He resisted arrest and, complaining of chest pains, was rushed to the hospital, where he died a few hours ago."

"Then how do you know he—"

"Keyes Hasting had some incriminating photographs taken at Erik Zander's Malibu beach house the night Camille Rush drowned in the hot tub and had apparently been blackmailing Mr. Zander. It would appear that Hasting had blackmailed him into doing the film."

Faith sat down on the edge of the bed. She felt Jud slide in behind her, his hands kneading her shoulder muscles. "He didn't say anything?" she asked dully.

"No. It appears he died of a heart attack," Carter said. "We found more evidence of the blackmail in Mr. Zander's trailer."

Faith was too shocked to think straight. She kept calling up images from the other night, something nagging at her. If only she could remember.

"So that's it." She tried to breathe a sigh of relief as she hung up the phone and told Jud what Carter had told her.

After their initial shock and disbelief passed, he said, "I'm just glad it's over." He pulled her to him.

Whatever had been nagging at her was forgotten the moment Jud kissed her.

NANCY CALLED to say that shooting would continue. "I know Erik would have wanted us to finish this film."

Jud had his doubts about that, given what the sheriff had told them confidentially. But since Nancy had been in charge of most everything to do with the film before Zander's death, she said finishing the film wouldn't be that hard given that they had only two more days of shooting.

"We'll shoot the rest of the stunts this afternoon," Nancy said. "I left a message on Faith's cell phone. If you see her, let her know."

"Will do," he said as Faith came out of the shower wrapped in a towel.

Jud told her what Nancy had said, still a little surprised. But then again, this was the movies. No time for sentiment.

He and Faith were still in shock over the earlier news about Hasting's murder and Erik Zander's death.

"Blackmail?" he repeated, not for the first time. "I still can't believe it."

"Apparently the photographs Hasting had of the night of the Malibu party where Camille Rush died were incriminating enough that Zander went along with the blackmail," Faith said as he watched her get dressed.

He would never get tired of looking at her. Or touching her. Or making love to her. In fact, right now, all he wanted to do was climb back into the bed with her. He would have been content just to hold her.

"Didn't I hear that you were at that party?"

It took Jud a moment to shift gears. He nodded. "I left before it happened." He frowned. "Keyes Hasting wasn't at the party. So how did he get incriminating photographs?"

"Someone else at the party?" Faith suggested, sitting down on the edge of the bed next to him. "I found out something yesterday. This wasn't the first starlet connected to

Erik Zander who died. Over twenty years ago, another one died in a car wreck. Zander was allegedly drunk and driving and left the scene of the accident, but he was never charged for the woman's death. The death mirrors the one in the hot tub in that the woman was allegedly pregnant with his child."

"So you kept digging into things, didn't you?" Jud said.

Faith ignored him. "The woman had a daughter named Samantha Brooke Keifer. The daughter changed her name to Brooke Keith."

He sat up straighter in the bed. "You're telling me it was Brooke's mother?"

"Kind of a coincidence, wouldn't you say, given everything that's been going on?"

"You're not sorry I talked you into doing the stunts for this film even with everything that has happened?" Jud asked.

She shook her head and smiled over at him. "You made my dreams come true. I'll never forget that. Or forget you."

He swallowed, realizing that tomorrow the film would be over. And then what? "What are your plans after the film is over?"

Faith had known this day was coming and was ready. "Spend the rest of the summer here on the ranch helping my sisters," she said without hesitation. "McKenna has a horse ranch not far from here and Eve always needs help running the cattle ranch my parents left us. There's always plenty to do."

What she hadn't let herself think about was fall. She'd finished college with a liberal arts degree and no plan for the future. Because nothing but trick riding had interested her.

Doing the stunts on *Death at Lost Creek* had only made her more interested in trick riding. She just wasn't so sure she wanted to do movies. She loved Montana. This was home. Unlike Jud, she didn't like the moving-on part after a job was over.

"What about you?" she asked when he fell silent.

"I have another movie, this one being filmed in Wyoming down by Laramie. I was thinking that maybe I could see about getting you a job on the film."

She shook her head. "Thanks, but I don't think so." She couldn't imagine anything worse than trailing after Jud film after film. Better to end it later today after their last stunt, no matter how painful. Make their goodbyes short and sweet.

Faith glanced at the clock. "I suppose we better get going."

Jud seemed to hesitate as if there were something more he wanted to say. Whatever it was, he rose and without another word headed for the shower while she went down to make them something to eat before they left for the set.

THE AFTERNOON SHOOT went off without a hitch. Jud couldn't believe how professional Faith was or how talented. She did all but one of the stunts on the first take. He could tell that Nancy was pleased.

Nancy seemed different without Zander around—more confident, definitely in control. She'd pulled her hair back into a ponytail and, on closer inspection, appeared to be wearing makeup. Jud knew people dealt differently with tragedy, but Nancy seemed to be in awfully good spirits. Either that or she was trying hard to hide her shock and grief.

"You did a great job," Nancy told Faith when they went to Nancy's trailer to collect their pay. "Here you go." Nancy had their checks ready.

"Jud, as always," she said as she handed him an envelope.

She rose to shake their hands. "I added a little extra to both of your checks. Best of luck to you both."

As they stepped out of the trailer, Faith shot him a look. "Was that odd or was it just me?" she whispered.

"Very odd. I've never been paid more than I was contracted for per stunt."

"I meant Nancy," Faith whispered as they walked toward her trailer.

"She does seem to be in a fine mood. I think she likes calling the shots. Zander held her back. I think she's glad he's gone."

Jud realized everything had gone much smoother today than it had when Zander was directing. "Chantal even showed up on time and didn't complain. Nevada didn't scowl at me."

"It's as if a cloud was over this place before," Faith commented as they reached her trailer. "I just have to get my things. Fortunately, I didn't bring much out here." She seemed to hesitate and Jud feared he knew what was coming. "I think we should say goodbye now. Leave it on a high note."

Jud couldn't speak as she held out her hand to shake his. He took her hand and held it. "At least let me take you to dinner tonight to celebrate."

She shook her head. "Thank you, but I think this is best." She smiled then, her blue eyes shining. "See you in the movies." With that she extracted her hand from his and went into her trailer, closing the door behind her.

FAITH STOOD on the other side of the trailer door, fighting to hold back the tears. She had trouble catching her breath. She couldn't remember ever doing anything as hard as saying goodbye to Jud.

Her heart felt as if it would break into a million pieces. Each beat was a labor. How would she ever get over him?

She'd done the worst thing possible. She'd fallen in love with him. Hadn't she told herself not to? She knew from the get-go that Jud wasn't the staying type, let alone the marrying type. Neither was she, she reminded herself.

And yet now she finally understood what had happened to her friends, why they'd traded their dreams of adventure for a mortgage and diapers when they'd fallen in love.

Love. It changed everything.

She quickly packed up her few things, then, checking to make sure no one was around, she hurried to her pickup. Five miles down the road, she had to pull over, she was crying so hard.

"SO THAT'S THE END of that, huh?"

Jud turned to find Brooke standing behind him. He'd been sitting off by himself on an outcropping of rocks, staring out across the prairie. "Film's over," he said gruffly, wishing she'd leave him alone.

"I can see you're in a good mood," she said sarcastically. She sat down on a rock next to him. "It's not the first heart you've broken. She'll get over it."

He laughed and looked over at her. "What makes you think it's *her* heart that got broken?"

Brooke pulled back in mock surprise. "You have a heart?"

"Funny."

"Come on, Jud, this isn't like you," she said. "Finishing a film is always a letdown. You just need to get on to the next one. You won't even remember that little cowgirl."

He could have argued the point, but didn't. "No one seems very upset by what happened with Zander."

"It was a shock, but it's Hollywood. Maybe we're all

cynics or maybe we're just numb to this sort of thing." She shrugged. "You have to admit Nancy seems to be as good a director as Zander was, maybe better because she's sober during the day." Brooke laughed and nudged him. "Come on. I'll let you take me out to dinner tonight. The Corbett Code doesn't apply now that we don't work together."

He shook his head. "I'd make a lousy dinner companion, trust me. Anyway, I need to go out to the ranch. But maybe some other time. Are you heading to Wyoming for the next Western?"

She shook her head. "I'm taking some time off. Regrouping," she said, getting to her feet and brushing off her backside.

"Can I ask you something?" Jud said, looking up to her. "What was your mother's name?"

"Angie. Why?"

"Just curious. Angie Keith?"

"Yeah," she said and lied to his face. "But she changed her last name a lot. I lost count of all the stepfathers I had. Why would you want to know that?" Her eyes filled with suspicion.

"I thought you'd mentioned before that you had stepfathers," he said casually. "I have a stepmother now. It's a little strange. I call her Kate. But it turns out she has a daughter, so now I have a half sister. So what does that make her to me?"

Brooke laughed. "She's just a stepsister by marriage. Kids usually come with stepparents. How old is this stepsister?"

"My age. Instant relatives."

"Been there," Brooke said, seeming to relax. "One day you're an only child and the next day your new daddy's kids are moving in and taking your stuff and telling you what to do. It sucks, but it comes with the territory."

"It must have been hard growing up like that."

She shook it off. "What doesn't kill you makes you strong. Actually, it was okay having stepsisters. There's a bond between sisters. It's hard to explain. Even when you don't share the same blood. Good luck with your next gig. Maybe we'll see each other around."

"Maybe we will," he said, watching her walk away. His first instinct when Brooke was out of earshot was to call Faith. She'd want to know what he'd learned, wouldn't she?

As he keyed in the number, he didn't kid himself. It was just an excuse to hear her voice. Unfortunately, her voice mail picked up.

"Hey, it's me, Jud. I just talked to Brooke. I verified what you found out about her mother. Sounds like she had a rough life, lots of stepfathers and step-siblings. Bet she didn't have sisters like yours." He hesitated, wishing he'd waited to tell her all this. Now what would he use for an excuse to call her later?

JUST OVER THE NEXT RISE, Brooke listened to Jud's phone call, balling her hands into fists as she heard him click off.

Who had he called?

Faith.

She quickened her pace, not wanting him to catch up with her. She didn't want him to know she'd overheard his call.

As she reached the camp, she hurried to her trailer to deal with her disappointment.

She'd thought for sure that once the film shoot was over Jud would forget about his little cowgirl and be ready to move on to his next conquest.

Not that Brooke saw herself in that role. But why not? He'd never even asked her out. And what about his stupid

Corbett Code? He'd gone out with Faith. She knew for a fact that they'd spent the night together.

Her disappointment with Jud was almost too much to bear. He was acting as if he'd fallen in love with Faith. That wasn't possible, but she'd never seen him this despondent.

Letting out a cleansing breath, she straightened, dried her eyes and readied herself to go see Nancy and collect her money. She'd get over this and move on.

But as she left her trailer, she felt at loose ends. She hadn't expected having this over would be such a letdown, let alone having Jud disappoint her the way he had.

He didn't seem to understand what a good friend she was. Maybe she'd have to tell him, she thought bitterly as she walked through the quickly disappearing camp. But then, that would spoil everything. Better to let it go, right?

By this time tomorrow, no one would ever know they'd been here. That was the way it should be, Brooke thought as she knocked on Nancy's door. Here and gone.

Chapter Fourteen

"They're packing up and leaving," the deputy sheriff said when he reported in. "Looks like a damned carnival—everything loaded on trailers, and pulling out."

Sheriff Carter Jackson swore under his breath. The evidence had been collected. He had no reason to detain the film crew. Just a few loose ends to tie up and this case would be history.

He covered the mouthpiece with his hand and hollered in to the office. "Any word from the coroner on the autopsy or from the crime lab on that DNA test?"

"Not yet," the clerk called back.

"Let them leave. We have no reason to hold them," Carter said.

As he hung up, he told himself that he had Keyes Hasting's killer. All the evidence pointed directly to Erik Zander. Maybe that's what was bothering him. It was all too neat, right down to the director's heart attack.

Carter remembered his sister-in-law's reaction when he'd told her the killer was apparently Zander. She'd sounded doubtful. Something about all this was bothering her, as well. She'd seen the killer dragging the body away to an old pickup. Had she remembered something?

The crime team had gone over the pickups the film crew had rented for the shoot but found nothing. That damned rain had washed away any evidence. Everyone had access to the trucks, including Zander. He had motive and opportunity. He'd tried to make a run for it when they'd gone to arrest him.

What more did Carter want?

He snatched up his phone on the first ring, hoping this was finally some good news. "Sheriff Jackson."

"Bad day?" It was his wife, Eve. His tone changed at just the sound of her voice.

"Not anymore." She'd been through so much lately and he'd missed it. He couldn't believe that she'd finally found her family. The change in her had been dramatic. Now maybe she could move on.

He'd been thinking about that. Sometimes this job got to him and he thought about going back to ranching so he could spend more time with Eve.

"Are you coming home for dinner?"

He groaned, suddenly aware of how late it was getting. "I have to wait for two reports on this Hasting murder. I'm sorry."

"McKenna and Nate have invited me over," Eve said. "Maybe I'll go if it's all right with you. If you get your reports early, you can join us."

"That sounds great. Have you told your sisters yet?"

"Not yet. But I will when the time is right."

He loved the serenity in her voice. Finding out about her mother had been painful but had released her. She now had a family that shared her blood. He knew how much that meant to her.

"I've been thinking," she said. "I know you're busy, but I think I'm ready to start a family."

He wanted to let out a whoop of joy. "Oh, Eve, I wish I could come home right now."

She chuckled. "Maybe after you get your reports…"

He hung up, happier than he could remember being.

FAITH CAME BACK from her ride and saw that Jud had called. She considered erasing the message without listening to it. After saying goodbye to Jud, she'd come straight to the ranch, saddled her horse and ridden deep into the Missouri Breaks.

But nothing would take away the ache inside her. Jud Corbett had broken down all her barriers. She'd opened herself up to him, knowing full well how it would end. At the time, she promised herself there would be no regrets.

But there were plenty of regrets.

Hadn't Brooke tried to warn her? *Don't take anything about movies seriously, especially Jud Corbett.*

Faith hesitated for a moment, then played Jud's message. He sounded odd, she thought. She played the message again, actually listening to his words and not trying to read something into his tone.

"Sisters?" *Bet she didn't have sisters like yours.* As Faith snapped the phone shut, she stood for a moment trying to understand why something was still nagging at her about Hasting's murder.

From where she stood, she could see the dark outline of the Little Rockies against the deepening darkness. Suddenly, she didn't want to be alone tonight. She picked up the phone and tapped in Eve's number. No answer.

"You're just being silly," she told herself as she walked out onto the porch. A breeze stirred the loose ends of her hair that had come free from her ponytail. She breathed in the night air, the familiar scents making her feel a little better.

Carter is convinced he got Hasting's killer. It's over. By now the film crew has packed up and probably left town.

A hawk flew over, the rustle of wings and motion startling her. What was wrong with her? She wasn't usually this jumpy. Faith chuckled at the thought. Why wouldn't she feel vulnerable? She'd seen a murderer, gotten so close he'd not only seen her, he'd struck her. She shivered at the thought.

Zander was dead. She was safe. So why did she feel so anxious? *Because you let yourself fall in love with Jud Corbett.*

That's what she'd done all right. Fallen for the arrogant, handsome, funny, charming stuntman.

Shaking her head, she went back into the house and did something she'd never done before. She locked the door behind her. Whatever had her keyed up tonight, whether it was murder or love, she wasn't taking any chances.

"You're awfully quiet tonight," Dalton Corbett said as he joined his brother Jud in the family room at Trails West.

Jud stared out at the growing darkness. The outline of the Little Rockies was etched black against the coming night. He wondered if Faith was looking out at the mountains, as well.

"Jud?" Dalton gave him a nudge.

"Sorry. What?"

Dalton laughed. "I was hoping you were bringing that adorable cowgirl you brought to dinner the other night. You look as if she dumped you."

Jud smiled at that. "She did."

"*Sure* she did."

Juanita called them in to dinner. Jud wasn't hungry, but he rose with the others and wandered into the huge dining room. He could smell the chile verde, warm homemade tortillas, pinto beans and bits of ham simmering in a pot on the table and his stomach growled. *Traitor.*

The conversation around the table was lively, his family in good spirits. Jud knew it was because Maddie was here with Shane. The wedding was on. Maddie and Kate seemed to be working out their differences. His father couldn't have looked happier.

"Finally a wedding," Lantry said and grinned over at Jud. "Let me see, who's next? Oh that's right, wasn't it Jud who drew the shortest straw?"

Everyone laughed but Jud. He looked around the table at all the smiling faces and felt worse than he had earlier. As food was passed to him, he filled his plate, but every bite tasted like cardboard—not that he would tell Juanita that. She'd hit him with the plate of tortillas.

"So where's your next movie?" Kate asked, studying him.

"Wyoming. But I have a few weeks before it begins." He filled a tortilla with chile verde and took a bite.

"Good," his father said. "You can stay with us for a while." Grayson beamed.

"You can help plan Shane and Maddie's wedding," Russell joked.

"I haven't decided what I'm going to do just yet," Jud said and saw his stepmother studying him again with a look of compassion as if she recognized heartbreak and felt for him.

"Tell us about the murder investigation," Lantry said.

Normally Kate would have objected to such a discussion at the dinner table. Jud was glad she didn't, grateful for a change of subject. He told them what he could.

"Faith *saw* the killer?" Kate said, her hand going to her throat.

Jud nodded. "He struck her with something. If she hadn't gotten away…and if I hadn't seen her wandering through the camp…" He didn't want to think about that.

"Well, she must be glad the killer isn't still out there," Kate said.

Jud nodded, remembering how Faith had questioned the sheriff. She hadn't believed the killer was Zander. He felt a tightening in his stomach. He found himself on his feet.

"Jud?" His father's voice.

"Is everything all right?" Kate asked.

"No—that is, I'm not sure. I just have this feeling." He glanced around the table to find them all staring at him. "I have to go. I'm sorry. I don't have time to explain." He threw down his napkin and headed for his pickup.

CORONER RALPH BROWN called just as Carter was about to give up and go join his wife at dinner with her sister and brother-in-law.

"Sorry it took so long, Sheriff," Ralph said. "We've been waiting for the results of the lab tests."

"And?"

"Erik Zander had a drug in his system called meta-belazene, which constricts the blood vessels. In large doses it causes labored breathing, dizziness, confusion and death."

"Doc said Zander had been in the emergency room earlier this week with what had appeared to be a panic attack. But he ran lab tests. Wouldn't he have found this metabelazene if that's what it was?"

"Not necessarily. I doubt they tested for it. It's a new drug. It's often given for snakebite victims."

Carter felt his pulse jump. The moment he hung up, he called Doc over at the hospital. "I need to ask you a quick question. Did you give Brooke Keith metabelazene for her rattlesnake bite?"

Doc sighed. "You know I can't—"

"Do you usually prescribe metabelazene for snakebites, just tell me that."

"Yes, it's the most effective new drug we've found, but you have to be careful because of the side effects and too much of it, of course, can kill a person."

Carter hung up and, grabbing his hat, headed for the door.

SHERIFF JACKSON TOPPED the hill overlooking where the film crew had camped. The set was gone and so were all of the equipment trailers and trucks, most of the residential trailers. Only three remained.

His cell phone rang. He stopped his patrol SUV, killing the headlights as he took the call. It was one of the techs at the crime lab, working late.

"The DNA from the doll brought up a name," the tech said. "I thought you'd want to know right away."

"Someone with a record?"

"You guessed it. A small-time crook named John Crane. He's serving time in California for robbery."

"He's in prison. Then how—"

"The DNA wasn't a perfect match, but close enough that it has to be one of his siblings. A sister."

"Sister?" Carter echoed.

"Half sister would be my guess. You know, with all these mixed families anymore…"

A half sister. "So you're saying that the blood on that doll belongs to a half sister of this John Crane. So she probably doesn't share the same last name."

"With the blending of families you end up with lots of different last names unless the stepfather adopts the children. Add to that all the couples who are blending families without the benefit of marriage and there is no record of these relationships."

Which meant Carter was back to square one. Not quite, he reminded himself. He knew Zander had been murdered. He also knew the blood from the doll was a woman's and Brooke Keith had been given the same drug for her snakebite that had been used to murder Zander. He also knew she had a motive for killing the director—her mother's death all those years ago.

"Sorry I couldn't be of more help."

"No, I appreciate you staying on this for me. Thanks." Hanging up, Carter turned on his headlights again and drove down into what was left of the camp.

He wondered why three trailers were still here and noted that there were only two vehicles. He parked and walked toward the first trailer. Voices rose up out of the darkness. As he neared the trailer, he saw a campfire blazing in the distance. Two people were standing by it, laughing and drinking.

He unsnapped his holster and moved toward them.

As he drew closer, he saw that the figures standing by the fire were two women. He recognized them from when he'd come out here questioning everyone about Keyes Hasting's possible disappearance.

Chantal Lee must have heard him approach. She turned from the fire to squint into the darkness, then seemed to start as she saw him. Immediately she checked her expression.

"Why, Sheriff, it's so good of you to join us," she said, and laughed as she held up the half-empty bottle of wine in her hand. "I hope you're not here to arrest us for being drunk and disorderly. We're just celebrating the end of the film. It's a tradition."

"You're sure you're not celebrating Erik Zander's death?" Carter asked, directing his question to the other woman standing by the fire.

Brooke Keith raised her gaze slowly. He saw contempt in the stuntwoman's gaze. She said nothing, just seemed to be waiting.

Hadn't Faith mentioned something to Eve about the two women hating each other? And yet here they were.

"I suppose you could say this is a wake for poor Erik, as well," Chantal said. "You know, I was afraid he'd had a heart attack that other time, when the doctor said it was nothing more than a panic attack. The man was under a great deal of stress."

"He didn't die of a heart attack," Carter said.

"Really?" Chantal sounded genuinely surprised.

"He was murdered."

She gasped, covering her mouth as her gaze shifted to Brooke standing across the blaze from her. A look passed between them.

"Do you still have the drugs you were given for your snakebite, Ms. Keith?" he asked.

"I don't. I didn't need them anymore, so I threw the remainder away. Are you telling me someone dug them out of the trash?"

Carter could see how this was going down. Unless he had hard evidence, there would never be a conviction. The problem was, he thought, as he looked back and forth between the two of them, he wasn't sure who had actually killed Hasting—or Zander.

He glanced behind him toward the trailers. Three still left, and only two vehicles. "Who is staying in the third trailer?" he asked, suddenly apprehensive.

"Nancy Davis, the assistant director," Chantal said. "It

wouldn't be a celebration without her." They both laughed, clearly an inside joke.

He started to turn back to them, sensing that he'd made a terrible mistake. The blow took his feet out from under him. He heard the crack of the piece of firewood as it connected with his head, felt the repercussions rattle through him and the surprise when he found himself staring up at the stars.

"What the hell did you do that for? Now we're going to have to get rid of him, too," he heard one of them say just before everything went black.

FAITH MADE herself a peanut butter and chokecherry jelly sandwich, eating it standing in the well-lit kitchen. She wasn't hungry, but she knew she had to eat.

She kept thinking about Jud's phone call. She thought about calling him back on the pretense of wanting to discuss what he'd learned from Brooke.

Erik Zander had been responsible for Brooke's mother's death and now Zander, labeled a murderer for Hasting's death, was dead himself. How just things had turned out after all these years.

Was that what bothered her? She couldn't seem to get out of her head the images from the night she'd seen the killer dragging away Hasting's body. Something was wrong.

And not just with that night. Nancy's reaction when Faith had asked about Ashton, Idaho, and Brooke. Chantal and Brooke's rivalry. The accidents on the set. Nevada and Chantal.

There were always undercurrents on any film, but nothing like on *Death at Lost Creek*. And amazingly as if by magic, they'd all gone away the moment Zander was dead and Nancy took over to finish the film. The only person with a possible grudge against Zander had been

Brooke and yet she, of all of them, seemed the least affected by his death.

So what did it all mean, if anything? Faith shook her head, suspecting all her nagging doubts were just her way of diverting her attention away from thinking about Jud. As if that were possible. Every heartbeat reminded her that he was gone.

Faith took a hot bath, hoping to relieve some of her tension. She'd never been afraid in this house, but tonight she'd locked all the doors and had been tempted to check every closet. She couldn't understand her unease.

Filling the tub, she stripped down and slipped into the warm, sudsy water. The water lapped over her naked body. Images of making love with Jud rushed at her. She ducked her head under the water, holding her breath until she couldn't anymore.

Bursting out of the water, she heard something. A creak. Old houses always creaked. But this creak was more like a slow, furtive footstep on a lower stair. After all these years in the house, Faith knew which stairs creaked the loudest.

She brushed her wet hair back from her face and listened. Another creak. Rising out of the bath as quietly as possible, she toweled off and pulled on her robe. She'd left the bathroom door open and now edged toward it. Stopping, she listened.

Another creak below. Someone was sneaking up the stairs.

Frantically, Faith looked around the bathroom for something she could use as a weapon. She'd never used hairspray, didn't keep anything more lethal than an emery board in the medicine cabinet and knew digging out the blow dryer from the bottom cabinet would take too much time—and make too much noise. Also, it didn't make much of a weapon.

Her mind was racing. All her earlier anxiety came back to her. She'd been jumpy because she'd known this wasn't over. It hadn't been Erik Zander who'd dragged Hasting away from the camp. But how did she know that?

It didn't matter now, she told herself. Her cell phone was downstairs in her purse. There was no landline in her bedroom. She had to find a weapon she could use.

Something in the bedroom. Maybe the lamp next to her bed. Or a bookend from the shelf next to it.

She stepped around the door and into her bedroom. And froze.

The only light came from the lamp beside her bed. It cast a golden glow over the bed with its white chenille bedspread and brightly colored pillows.

Faith let out an involuntary gasp at the sight.

The doll sat against one of the pillows, its grotesque face staring out at her. But it wasn't the doll that made her take a step back, stumbling into the wall.

It was the person standing next to her bed.

"Nancy?" Faith said, trying to catch her breath. Her thumping heart threatened to bust out of her chest. All she could think was, *I should have checked the closets.* "What are you…" The rest of her words died on her lips as she saw the gun the woman held.

"You have to come with me," Nancy said calmly, as if there was a stunt that needed to be shot. "Please don't make this more difficult than it has to be."

"Where?"

"To a party," she said.

Faith stared at the woman. Was she insane? "A *party*?" Obviously a party requiring Nancy hold a gun on her to get her to go.

"Your brother-in-law the sheriff is there waiting.

Wouldn't it be awful if something happened to him? I know how close you are."

"You're lying."

"Am I? You really want to take that chance? If you want your sister ever to see him again do as I tell you. Get dressed."

Her head was whirling. This was just a bad dream, that's why it didn't make any sense.

"Hurry."

Outside, Faith saw one of the pickups Nancy had rented for the movie. Just like the one she'd seen that night at the dry creek bed.

"I don't understand why you're doing this," Faith said as she slid into the passenger seat.

"Sure you do," Nancy said as she slammed the door and walked around to climb behind the wheel. "You're an eye-witness in Keyes Hasting's murder."

Faith shook her head. "I didn't see Zander, or if I did, I can't remember." She touched the healed cut on her temple.

But hadn't she known Zander didn't kill Hasting? She hadn't seen him that night. But who had she seen? Nancy? Is that what this was about? Nancy was afraid she'd remember?

"What have you done with the sheriff?"

"You'll see," Nancy said. "Just remember, if you try anything, he dies."

Faith stared at the road ahead as Nancy drove, the gun resting on her lap.

She refused to let her earlier fear paralyze her. She had to keep her wits about her if she had any hope of getting out of this.

THE NIGHT WAS unusually dark. Wind blew over the tall green grass beside the road as Jud drove his pickup toward

Faith's ranch house. He felt a sense of urgency he couldn't explain. Nothing made sense. All he knew was that he had to get to Faith.

Just this morning he'd awakened in her bed. He smiled at the memory. He wanted to wake in her bed every morning for the rest of their lives.

That thought made him laugh out loud, because it was one he'd believed he would never give voice to. He *loved* her. He wanted to scream it to the heavens. It was amazing that Jud Corbett had fallen in love. Wait until he told his family.

His fear kicked up a notch at the thought that the woman he loved and wanted to share the rest of his life with was in mortal danger. He felt it as intensely as he felt his love for her.

He was already going too fast, but he sped up. His mind raced as he began to see a pattern. The accidents on the set. Hasting's death. Zander's heart attack.

Was it possible?

Fear seized him as he realized what it was about Faith's story that had nagged at her. The tailgate on the pickup she'd seen in the dry creek bed. The killer had put it down after backing up to the embankment.

Zander wouldn't have had to do that. He was a big man. Hasting was small, a lightweight. Zander could easily have tossed him into the truck bed.

But someone smaller, say a woman…

He took the last curve a little too fast. Ahead he could see the Bailey Ranch house. Faith's pickup was parked out front and a light burned upstairs in one of the windows. Her bedroom window.

There was nothing to fear. She was safe in her bed. She would think him a complete fool for rushing over here, scaring her.

Jud swore as he tore into the ranch yard and jumped out, taking the porch stairs two at a time. To hell with worrying about looking like a fool. The bad feeling he'd felt at dinner was full-blown now.

The front door was unlocked. "Faith!" He charged up the stairs. "Faith!" He heard nothing over the pounding of his heart and his boots on the stairs. *"Faith!"*

Her bedroom light was on. So was the bathroom light, the door open. The scent of fresh soap and humidity hung in the air. He could see her robe lying in a heap on the bathroom floor as if she'd just dropped it there.

Faith was gone.

It wasn't until that moment that Jud saw the doll. It was propped up against a pillow—just like all the others that had been discovered on the set.

"Son of a—"

The set. If Zander hadn't killed Hasting, then—

He ran down the stairs, the doll clutched in his hand. He tossed it on his pickup seat and took off down the road toward Lost Creek.

"THE LEAST YOU CAN DO is tell me what all this is about," Faith said as they drove through the darkness.

Nancy shot her a disbelieving look. "Come on, girl detective, you spent all that time digging into our lives. Surely you've figured it out by now."

Had she? "I know about Brooke's mother and Zander. But where does Keyes Hasting fit in?"

Nancy smiled, pleased that Faith wasn't as smart as she thought she was. "His goddaughter was Camille Rush."

"The young woman who drowned in Zander's hot tub?"

"He financed the film as a way to get Erik Zander not just to Montana, but to Lost Creek for us. That was his part.

I'd read about the legend of Lost Creek in one of my step-father's real-life mystery magazines. The setting was perfect. A vengeful father against an entire town."

Or in this case against Hollywood and the establishment in the form of Erik Zander. "Hasting got Zander to do the movie by blackmailing him and picked the cast and crew."

Nancy smiled over at her. "You really are a girl detective, aren't you?"

"So the accidents on the set were for, let me guess, simply setting the stage, building tension so Zander's heart attack wouldn't be questioned?"

"Damn, girl, you are good."

Faith realized where they were headed. Lost Creek. She should have known. *Death at Lost Creek,* and this plot against Zander was all about symbolism.

"Seems like a lot of trouble for a simple case of revenge."

"It was a whole lot more than that," Nancy snapped. "Zander needed to suffer. He thought *Death at Lost Creek* was going to save him. But before he died he came to realize it was his own death he'd been cast in."

"But why kill Hasting?"

"He'd served his purpose and we needed to frame Zander for his murder. Justice had to be done."

She'd said "we." Just as Faith had suspected, Nancy hadn't acted alone.

"You think killing me is just?" Faith demanded.

"You're collateral damage."

"I can understand how Brooke might want revenge against Erik Zander for her mother's death, but what does any of this have to do with you?" Faith asked as Nancy slowed at the top of the hill overlooking what had been the set. Everything was gone but three trailers. Past them a light burned in the dark night. A fire?

As the pickup bumped down the hill to park next to one of the trailers, Faith spotted a vehicle parked beside one of the trailers. Sheriff Jackson's patrol SUV. Nancy hadn't been lying.

Faith knew this was her chance.

She grabbed the gun, slapping away Nancy's hand as she made a grab for it, and bolted out of the pickup at a run.

"Carter!" she cried as she ran toward the light.

Behind her she heard Nancy get out of the truck. She'd expected Nancy to leave, to make a break for it. Why was she following Faith, who had the gun now?

As she ran past the trailers, Faith saw two dark figures standing around a bonfire. Neither was the right size to be Carter. So where was he?

"Faith?" Chantal said, looking surprised to see her. Or maybe she was surprised to see her holding a gun on them.

"Where is the sheriff?"

Faith heard Nancy approaching the fire and turned the pistol on her. "What have you done with Carter?"

"I see you've met my sisters," Nancy said.

"Sisters?" Faith echoed, distracted for a moment too long.

"Stepsisters," Chantal said, shoving something cold and hard into Faith's back. "Isn't that a bitch?"

THE PICKUP BUMPED over the rough terrain, jarring Faith painfully as she lay on the hard metal truck bed. Her wrists and ankles were tied with rope that was cutting off her circulation. Next to her, Carter groaned as he slowly came awake. His hair was caked with blood and when she'd first seen him, she'd thought he was dead and had almost lost it.

"Faith?" He swallowed, licked his lips and looked around.

"They're taking us to the ghost town," she whispered,

not sure the three in the front of the pickup couldn't hear them. It could work to their advantage that they didn't know Carter had regained consciousness.

He closed his eyes for a moment as they were both jostled when the pickup hit a bump. "Turn your back to me. Maybe I can get you untied."

She did as he instructed and felt his fingers working at the knots.

"It's all three of them, isn't it?" he said.

"They're stepsisters. They were just fighting over who got to drive the pickup and who got to ride next to the window."

"No wonder it appeared they didn't like each other."

"At least that part wasn't an act. They don't know you're awake yet." She felt the rope binding her wrists loosen and she was able to free one hand, then the other.

Faith swung around and worked frantically to untie Carter's hands.

"Get your ankles free," he said as the pickup began to slow. "There isn't time to untie me. Jump down and run."

She worked faster. "I'm not leaving you."

"You have to. It's our only chance. *Go!*"

The pickup engine groaned as it came to a stop.

Faith scrambled to her feet and leaped off the back of the pickup, hitting the ground running. The dark night swallowed her as she sprinted down the track, the light of the bonfire flickering in the distance.

If she could get to Carter's patrol SUV, she could call for help. There would also be a shotgun in the patrol car. The shotgun would be loaded.

JUD STOPPED on the other side of the hill from where the movie camp had been and turned off the engine. Getting out, he took the .22 rifle he carried from behind his pickup seat. Every rancher's kid had one for gopher hunting. Gophers dug holes that horses stepped in. Like most places in these parts, Whitehorse had a yearly gopher hunt to get rid as many of the varmints as possible in one day.

As Jud started out, he wished he had a more powerful weapon with him. The varmints he was hunting tonight would be much larger, much harder to kill.

He topped the hill, staying low, glad for the darkness. He could see three trailers, all dark inside, below in the prairie and three vehicles. Nearby, a fire burned, but there was no sign of anyone around it.

So where was everyone? He just hoped to hell his instincts were right as he dropped on down the hillside and sneaked along one of the trailers. When he got close enough to the SUV, he was startled to see that it was a sheriff's department vehicle.

His apprehension intensified. Something was very wrong here.

He moved to the next trailer, staying to the dark shadows, listening for any sign of life.

The sound of a gunshot ripped through the air. He heard a cry in the distance, then voices. From the direction of the ghost town, pickup brake lights flashed on as an engine cranked over. As the truck swung around in this direction, he ducked down instinctively.

The glow of the headlights washed over the open prairie between him and the ghost town behind the truck. That's when he saw Faith. She was running toward him, holding her side.

It took him an instant to realize what was happening as the sound of another shot filled the night air. The bullet kicked up earth next to Faith in the pickup's headlights as the truck barreled after her, engine roaring.

Jud raised his .22 rifle and aimed for the pickup's front tire. Like shooting fish in a barrel. The tire blew. The pickup rocked crazily in the rutted dirt track, then veered off, headed for the river.

Jud saw a shape rise from the back of the truck and jump free just an instant before the pickup plunged into the Missouri. And then Jud was on his feet, running toward Faith.

She had stumbled and fallen near the bonfire. He ran to her, dropping to his knees. The firelight caught her beautiful face and he saw at once how pale she was.

"Faith," he cried as he saw that she was still clutching her side, her shirt and hand soaked in blood. "Oh, my God." He swept her up into his arms as Sheriff Jackson came running toward him. "She's been shot."

Faith smiled up at him, then at Carter. "I'm fine. Don't worry about me. Get the stepsisters. You can't let them get away," she said, then passed out in Jud's arms.

Chapter Fifteen

"You have a very tough girl there," the doctor said when he came out to tell everyone how Faith was doing. "Fortunately, the bullet didn't hit any organs. She's awake, if you want to see her now."

"I need to see her first," Jud said as the two families started to get to their feet. *"Alone."* He'd been so afraid he would lose her. The thought that she wouldn't know how he felt about her was unbearable—no matter how she felt about him.

He turned to his family and Eve's. They'd filled the waiting room to overflowing. "I'm in love with Faith and I'm going to marry her," he blurted out.

"As if that wasn't obvious," Eve said, to his surprise.

"Don't you think you'd better ask her first?" his brother Shane said.

"Yeah, she might not want you," Dalton agreed.

"Maybe you should give this a little more thought," Russell suggested. The oldest of the brothers was always the most sensible. The women in the room, Maddie, Kate, Eve, McKenna and Juanita, booed him.

Everyone else laughed, Jud along with them. "Nothing is going to change my mind. There is no one like Faith. Just give me a minute alone with her. Please? This really can't wait."

Kate and his father were smiling knowingly.

"Make it quick," Eve said, only half joking. "We want to see for ourselves that she's all right."

Jud smiled at his sister-in-law-to-be. "Wish me luck?"

"You don't need luck," Eve said. "You have love."

Faith was lying in the bed. The color had come back into her face. Her eyes were that incredible blue that would always remind him of Montana summer days.

"Hi," he said, feeling strangely awkward. This woman had always thrown him off-kilter, leaving his spinning, from the first. She would give him a run for his money the rest of his days—just as she had on the dance floor, he realized and grinned at the thought. He was ready for the challenge.

FAITH SMILED as Jud tugged off his Western hat and sidled into the room, looking shy and sweet. The man took her breath away and had from the first day she'd laid eyes on him.

"You've been making a habit of saving my life," she said, then she turned serious. "Thank you."

Jud moved to her bed to take her hand. She watched him swallow and could feel how nervous he was. "There's something I have to tell you. I love you."

Faith felt her heart swell at his words, knowing these were not words Jud Corbett had ever said to another woman. "I love you, too."

He broke out in a big grin. "I can't tell you how happy I am to hear you say that, because I can't stand the thought of spending another day without you. Marry me, Faith. Make me the happiest damned cowboy in Montana."

She laughed through her tears. "There is nothing more that I'd rather do, but, Jud, I know how much you love being a stuntman, and I've realized that life really isn't for me."

He nodded. "I gave that a lot of thought while I was

waiting out there in the hallway to find out whether you were going to live or die, and I think I have a plan you're going to like."

CARTER STUCK his head in the hospital-room door. "Well?" he asked.

Jud gave him a thumbs-up.

Carter stepped in. "I need to talk to Faith for a few minutes, and her sisters are about to start a riot out there."

Jud squeezed Faith's hand. "I need to go buy an engagement ring."

"Make it two simple gold bands," Faith said. "I've never been a diamond kind of girl."

Carter shook Jud's hand as he was leaving. "You saved our lives last night. Thank you."

"What happened to them?" Faith asked her brother-in-law when they were alone. He knew she was talking about Nancy, Chantal and Brooke.

"We found three bodies in the cab of the pickup. They drowned together." He shook his head. "It's crazy. I swear they despised each other, and yet they came up with this scheme to bring down a killer," he said.

"So they really were sisters?"

"Stepsisters. I heard them arguing as they were chasing you. I'm surprised they didn't kill each other. Brooke knew she was allergic to metabelazene snake antidote and yet she still let that snake bite her so she could get the medicine needed to kill Erik Zander."

"They cooked it up among themselves?" she asked.

"Nancy was the leader, from what I could tell. She planned it, but the others went along with it. It isn't even a case of blood being thicker than water."

Faith was stunned.

"The woman Zander let drown in the car accident twenty-three years ago was Brooke's mother and Chantal's and Nancy's stepmother," Carter said. "When that other young woman drowned in a hot tub at Zander's party earlier this year, they hatched this plot with Camille Rush's godfather. It's crazy, but then revenge is, isn't it? Still, I'm amazed those three women were able to almost pull it off. If you hadn't seen one of them dragging away Hasting's body…"

Faith thought of her own sisters and the bond between them. "What about the dolls?"

"Scraps of material were found in Nancy Davis's place in California, but I suspect the three made the dolls together," Carter said. "They couldn't depend on being able to use the doll props once they got to the location shoot, I guess."

The door opened. "Time's up," Eve said. "You can get her statement later. She isn't going anywhere."

The sisters gathered around Faith's bed as Carter left the room, all three of them crying as they hugged and held hands.

"I'm so glad that you're my sisters," Faith said through her tears.

Eve nodded agreement. "There's something I need to tell the two of you."

Faith thought at once of the woman dressed in green that she'd seen on the movie set. The woman who resembled Eve.

"You know I've been searching for my birth mother," Eve said. "Well, I've found my birth family."

"Oh, sis, I'm so happy for you!" McKenna cried.

Faith echoed her sentiments and listened as Eve told her about her aunt Mary Ellen coming to Whitehorse after a call Eve had made during her search.

"My mother and father are gone, but I have a grandmother and an aunt," Eve said, and they were all three crying again.

"So when do we get to meet them?" McKenna wanted to know.

"Soon," Eve said. "They're coming the first part of August. I can't wait to meet my grandmother and for you to meet them, since we're all family, aren't we?"

"The more the merrier," McKenna said with a laugh. "And on that note, I'd like you two to be the first ones to know... I'm pregnant!"

A cheer rose up in the hospital room.

"I guess while we're all making announcements," Faith said. "Jud and I are getting married and we're going to start our own stunt school here in Whitehorse, and we were wondering—"

Eve laughed. "I thought you would never ask. Of course you can have it on the ranch. One-third of the Bailey Ranch is yours, and I know how you feel about the house. We've always known that you would come back here someday and live in it."

Faith laughed. "Actually, I was going to ask you if you'd be my matrons of honor, but you're right, I want to live in the house. There's so many memories there." Those memories were in every creaking board of that old house. Good memories stayed in a place just like bad ones, she thought, thinking of Lost Creek.

"This calls for a toast," McKenna said, and poured them each a plastic cup of water. She lifted her cup. "To the Bailey girls."

"To the *wild* Bailey girls," Faith said, and they all three clinked plastic cups.

* * * * *

In honor of our 60th anniversary,
Harlequin® American Romance® is celebrating
by featuring an all-American male each month,
all year long with
MEN MADE IN AMERICA!
This June, we'll be featuring American men
living in the West.

Here's a sneak preview of
THE CHIEF RANGER by Rebecca Winters.

Chief Ranger Vance Rossiter has to confront the sister
of a man who died while under Vance's watch...
and also confront his attraction to her.

"Chief Ranger Rossiter?" The sight of the woman who'd stepped inside Vance's office brought him to his feet. "I'm Rachel Darrow. Your secretary said I should come right in."

"Please," he said, walking around his desk to shake her hand. At a glance he estimated she was in her midtwenties. Her feminine curves did wonders for the pale blue T-shirt and jeans she was wearing. "Ranger Jarvis informed me there's a young boy with you."

The unfriendly expression in her beautiful green eyes caught him off guard. "Yes" was her clipped reply. "When we arrived in Yosemite the ranger told me I couldn't go anywhere in the park until I talked to you first."

"That's right."

"Knowing you wanted this meeting to be private, he offered to show my nephew around Headquarters."

So this woman was the victim's sister…. "What's his name?"

"Nicky."

The boy who haunted Vance's dreams now had a name. "How old is he?"

"He turned six three weeks ago. Were you the man in charge when my brother and sister-in-law were killed?"

"Yes. To tell you I'm sorry for what happened couldn't begin to convey my feelings."

The woman's gaze didn't flicker. "I won't even try to describe mine. Just tell me one thing. Was their accident preventable?"

"Yes," he answered without hesitation.

"In other words, the people working under you fell asleep on your watch and two lives were snuffed out as a result."

Hearing it put like that, he had to set the record straight. "My staff had nothing to do with it. I, myself, could have prevented the loss of life."

Ms. Darrow's expression hardened. "So you admit culpability."

"Yes. I take full blame."

A look of pain crossed over her features. "You can just stand there and admit it?" Her cry echoed that of his own tortured soul.

"Yes." He sucked in his breath.

"I work for a cruise line. Aboard ship, it's the captain's responsibility to maintain rigid safety regulations. If a disaster like that had happened while he was in charge he would have been relieved of his command and never given another ship again."

Rachel Darrow couldn't know she was preaching to the converted. "If you've come to the park with the intention of bringing a lawsuit against me for negligence, maybe you should." It would only be what he deserved.

"Maybe I will."

In the next instant, she wheeled around and hurried out of his office. Vance could have gone after her, but it would cause a scene, something he was loath to do for a variety of reasons. In the first place, he needed to cool down before he approached her again.

The discovery of the Darrows' frozen bodies had affected every ranger in the park. A little boy had been orphaned—a boy whose aunt was all he had left.

* * * * *

Will Rachel allow Vance to explain—
and will she let him into her heart?
Find out in
THE CHIEF RANGER
Available June 2009 from
Harlequin® American Romance®.

We'll be spotlighting a different series every month
throughout 2009 to celebrate our 60th anniversary.

Look for Harlequin®
American Romance® in June!

Join us for a year-long celebration of the rugged
American male! From cops to cowboys—
Men Made in America has the hero
you've been dreaming about!

Look for

The Chief Ranger

by Rebecca Winters, on sale in June!

Bachelor CEO by Michele Dunaway	July
The Rodeo Rider by Roxann Delaney	August
Doctor Daddy by Jacqueline Diamond	September

SPECIAL EDITION

FROM *USA TODAY* BESTSELLING AUTHOR

MARIE FERRARELLA

THE ALASKANS

LOVING THE RIGHT BROTHER

When tragedy struck, Irena Yovich headed
back to Alaska to console her ex-boyfriend's
family. While there she began seeing his brother,
Brody Hayes, in a very different light. Things
were about to really heat up. Had she fallen
for the wrong brother?

*Available in June
wherever books are sold.*

Escape Around the World

Dream destinations, whirlwind weddings!

Honeymoon with the Boss
by
JESSICA HART

Top tycoon Tom Maddison is used to calling the shots—until his convenient marriage falls through. But rather than waste his honeymoon, he'll take his boardroom to the beach and bring his oh-so-sensible secretary Imogen on a tropical business trip! But will Tom finally see the sexy woman that prudent Imogen truly is?

Available in June wherever books are sold.

Stay up-to-date on all your romance reading news!

The Inside Romance newsletter is a **FREE** quarterly newsletter highlighting our upcoming series releases and promotions!

Go to
eHarlequin.com/InsideRomance
or e-mail us at
InsideRomance@Harlequin.com
to sign up to receive
your **FREE** newsletter today!

REQUEST YOUR FREE BOOKS!

2 FREE NOVELS PLUS 2 FREE GIFTS!

HARLEQUIN® INTRIGUE®

Breathtaking Romantic Suspense

YES! Please send me 2 FREE Harlequin Intrigue® novels and my 2 FREE gifts (gifts are worth about $10). After receiving them, if I don't wish to receive any more books, I can return the shipping statement marked "cancel." If I don't cancel, I will receive 6 brand-new novels every month and be billed just $4.24 per book in the U.S. or $4.99 per book in Canada. That's a savings of close to 15% off the cover price! It's quite a bargain! Shipping and handling is just 50¢ per book.* I understand that accepting the 2 free books and gifts places me under no obligation to buy anything. I can always return a shipment and cancel at any time. Even if I never buy another book from Harlequin, the two free books and gifts are mine to keep forever.

182 HDN EYTR 382 HDN EYT3

Name	(PLEASE PRINT)	
Address		Apt. #
City	State/Prov.	Zip/Postal Code

Signature (if under 18, a parent or guardian must sign)

Mail to the **Harlequin Reader Service:**
IN U.S.A.: P.O. Box 1867, Buffalo, NY 14240-1867
IN CANADA: P.O. Box 609, Fort Erie, Ontario L2A 5X3

Not valid to current subscribers of Harlequin Intrigue books.

Are you a current subscriber of Harlequin Intrigue books and want to receive the larger-print edition? Call 1-800-873-8635 today!

* Terms and prices subject to change without notice. Prices do not include applicable taxes. Sales tax applicable in N.Y. Canadian residents will be charged applicable provincial taxes and GST. Offer not valid in Quebec. This offer is limited to one order per household. All orders subject to approval. Credit or debit balances in a customer's account(s) may be offset by any other outstanding balance owed by or to the customer. Please allow 4 to 6 weeks for delivery. Offer available while quantities last.

Your Privacy: Harlequin is committed to protecting your privacy. Our Privacy Policy is available online at www.eHarlequin.com or upon request from the Reader Service. From time to time we make our lists of customers available to reputable third parties who may have a product or service of interest to you. If you would prefer we not share your name and address, please check here. ☐

HI09R

You're invited to join our Tell Harlequin Reader Panel!

By joining our new reader panel you will:

- Receive Harlequin® books—they are FREE and yours to keep with no obligation to purchase anything!
- Participate in fun online surveys
- Exchange opinions and ideas with women just like you
- Have a say in our new book ideas and help us publish the best in women's fiction

In addition, you will have a chance to win great prizes and receive special gifts!
See Web site for details. Some conditions apply.
Space is limited.

To join, visit us at
www.TellHarlequin.com.

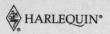